THE

CASTLE

in

Transylvania

The Castle in Transylvania

Serialized in *Le Magasin d'Éducation et de Récréation* and first published in France as *Le Château des Carpathes* by éditions Hetzel in 1892. First published in English as *The Castle of the Carpathians* by The Merriam Company in 1894.

© 2010 Melville House Publishing

Translation © 2010 Charlotte Mandell

Melville House Publishing
145 Plymouth Street
Brooklyn, NY 11201
www.mhpbooks.com

ISBN: 978-1-935554-08-0

Second Melville House Printing: January 2011

Book design by David Konopka

Printed in the United States of America

Library of Congress Control Number: 2010928523

THE CASTLE

in

Transylvania

Jules Verne

TRANSLATED BY CHARLOTTE MANDELL

MELVILLE HOUSE PUBLISHING
BROOKLYN, NEW YORK

I

This story is not fantastic; it is only romantic. Should we conclude that it isn't true, given its implausibility? That would be a mistake. We are living in a time when anything can happen—one can almost say, when everything has happened. If our tale is not very likely today, it can be so tomorrow, thanks to the scientific resources that are the lot of the future, so no one should take it into his head to rank it among legends. Moreover, legends have stopped being created in the decline of this practical and positive nineteenth century, even in Brittany, the country of the fierce Breton goblins, or in Scotland, the land of brownies and gnomes, or in Norway, the homeland of aesir, elves, sylphs and Valkyries, or even in Transylvania, where the setting of the Carpathians lends itself so readily to all psychagogic evocations. It should be noted, however, that Transylvania as a country is still quite attached to the superstitions of long ago.

Auguste de Gérando has described these provinces of outermost Europe—in his 1845 books *La Transylvanie et ses habitants*—and the geographer Jean-Jacques Élisée Reclus has visited them. Neither of them has said anything about the curious history on which this novel is based. Were they aware of it? Possibly, but they would surely refuse to give credence to it. That is regrettable, since they would have described it well—one with the precision of a historian, the other with that instinctive poetry that is the mark of his travel accounts.

Since neither one has told the story, I will try to do it for them.

On May 29 of the year in question, a shepherd was watching his herd on the edge of a green plateau at the foot of Mt. Retyezat, which towers over a fertile valley wooded with straight-trunked trees and enriched with fine plantations. This high, bare plateau, without any shelter, is shorn during the winter, as by a barber's razor, by the *galernes*, which are winds from the northwest. When that happens, country folk say that it's having its beard cut—and sometimes very closely.

There was nothing arcadian about this shepherd's attire, nor was there anything bucolic in his attitude. This was not Daphnis, Amyntas, Tityrus, Lycidas, or Melibeus. It wasn't the Loire that bubbled quietly at his clog-shod feet but rather the Wallachian Sil, whose fresh and pastoral waters would have been worthy of flowing through the twists and turns in Urfé's romance, *L'Astrée*.

Frik, Frik from the village of Werst—thus this rustic shepherd was named—as unkempt in his person as his animals, as he should be from living in that sordid hovel erected at the entrance to the village where his sheep and pigs lived in a revolting "verminry"—the only word, borrowed from the old language, fitting for the squalid sheepfolds of the district.

L'immanum pecus—the wild herd—were grazing, then, under the care of said Frik, *immanior ipse*—even wilder himself. Lying on a grassy mound, he slept with one eye and kept watch with the other, his big pipe in his mouth, sometimes whistling for his dogs when some sheep wandered away from the pasture, or sounding a horn that reverberated through the mountain.

It was four in the afternoon. The sun was beginning to set. A few peaks, whose bases were drowned in a floating mist, were lit up in the east. Near the southwest, two breaks in the mountain chain let a slanting beam of sunrays pass through, like a luminous shaft filtering through a half-open door.

This orographical system belonged to the wildest part of Transylvania, in the district of Klausenburg or Kolosvar, or Cluj.

A curious fragment of the Austrian empire, this Transylvania, "Erdely" in Magyar, or "the country of forests." It is bordered by Hungary to the north, Wallachia to the south, Moldavia to the west. Extending over 60,000 square kilometers, or six million hectares— almost a ninth of France—it's a kind of Switzerland, but twice as big as the Helvetian domain, without being more populated. With its cultivated plateaus, its luxuriant pastures, its capriciously outlined valleys, its haughty summits, Transylvania, streaked by the branches of the Carpathians, of plutonic origin, is furrowed by numerous watercourses that go on to swell the Theiss and the proud Danube, whose Iron Gates, a few miles south, close the procession of the Balkan chain on the border of Hungary and the Ottoman empire.

Such is the former country of the Dacians, conquered by Trajan in the first century of the Christian era. The independence it enjoyed under John Zapoly and his successors until 1699 came to an end with Leopold I, who annexed it to Austria. But, whatever its political constitution may have been, it remained the shared habitat of various races who rubbed elbows with each other without merging—the Wallachians or Romanians, Hungarians, the Gypsies, the Szeklers of Moldavian origin, and also the Saxons, whom time and circumstance ended up "Magyarizing" for the benefit of Transylvanian unity.

To what type did the shepherd Frik belong? Was he a degenerate descendant of the ancient Dacians? It would be hard to say, judging from his disheveled hair, his blackened face, his bushy beard, his thick eyebrows like two brushes with reddish hairs, his blue-green eyes, whose moist rims were surrounded by senile circles. That's because he is 65 years old—or at least there is reason to believe so. But he is tall, lean, upright beneath his yellowish sheepskin tunic less hairy than his chest, and a painter wouldn't scorn sketching his figure, when, wearing a woven hat made from real straw, he leans on his crow's-head crook, as motionless as a rock.

The instant the sun's rays penetrated the break in the west, Frik turned around; then, with his curled fingers, he fashioned a telescope for himself—just as he would have shaped it into a megaphone to be heard from afar—and he looked very attentively.

In the clearing on the horizon, a good mile away, but very much diminished by distance, the shapes of a citadel emerged. This ancient castle, on an isolated hill-top on the Vulkan Pass, occupied the upper part of a plateau called the Plateau of Orgall. In the play of a brilliant shaft of light, its outline was crudely articulated, with that sharpness stereoscopic views present. Still, the shepherd's eye had to have been endowed with a great power of vision to make out any detail in this distant mass.

Suddenly he cried out, shaking his head:

"Old citadel! Old citadel! In vain are you entrenched on your foundation! Three more years, and you'll have ceased to exist, since your beech tree has just three branches left!"

This beech tree, planted at the outermost part of one of the citadel's bastions, fitted its black shape over the background of the sky like a thin paper cutout, and it would have been barely visible to anyone but Frik at that distance. As to the explanation of the shepherd's words, which were provoked by a legend having to do with the castle, it will be given in time.

"Yes!" he repeated, "Three branches.... There were four yesterday, but the fourth fell overnight.... Just the stump remains.... I can count only three where the trunk forks.... No more than three, old citadel... no more than three!"

When we make an ideal image of a shepherd, our imagination readily creates a dreamy, contemplative being; he converses with the planets; he confers with the stars; he reads the heavens. In fact, generally he is a stupid, dense boor. But the credulity of the public easily attributes to him the gift of the supernatural; he knows evil spells; according to his humor, he wards off bad luck or sends it to people and animals—which is all the same in that case; he sells sympathetic powders; people buy potions and formulas from him. Doesn't he even make plowed furrows unfertile by throwing enchanted stones into them, and make sheep barren just by looking at them with his left eye? These superstitions belong to all times and all countries. Even in the midst of the most civilized countrysides, you can't pass by a shepherd without addressing some friendly word to him, some significant greeting, saluting him with the name "shepherd" to which he is partial. A tip of the hat allows you to escape from evil influences, and on the paths of Transylvania, one isn't spared them any more than elsewhere.

Frik was regarded as a sorcerer, an evoker of fantastic apparitions. According to one person, vampires and witches obeyed him; according to another, one could see him, as the moon was setting, on dark nights, as one sees the great bissext in other countries, astride the weir of a watermill, chatting with wolves or dreaming of the stars.

Frik let people talk, finding it to his advantage. He sold charms and counter-charms. But it should be noted that he himself was as credulous as his clientele, and if he didn't believe in his own spells, at least he had faith in the legends that traversed the country.

We will not be surprised, then, that he had made this prediction about the imminent disappearance of the old citadel, since the beech tree was reduced to three branches, or that he was eager to report this news to Werst.

After gathering his herd together by bellowing heartily through a long horn made of pinewood, Frik took the path to the village. His dogs followed him, pestering the animals—two mongrel half-griffons, vicious and fierce, who seemed more likely to devour the sheep than guard them. There were about a hundred rams and sheep, including a dozen or so year-old lambs, with the rest of the animals in their third or fourth year, or else with four or six teeth.

This herd belonged to the judge of Werst, Biró Koltz, who paid the district a large pasturage fee, and who had great appreciation for his shepherd Frik, knowing him to be very good at shearing, and very knowledgeable about treatment of illnesses: thrush, bluetongue, turnsick, vertigo, liver fluke, waterbelly, pink eye, sheep-pox, foot and mouth disease, scrapie, and other diseases of animal origin.

The herd walked in a compact formation, the belled ram in front, and, next to it, the leading ewe, making their bells tinkle in the midst of the bleating.

Leaving the pasture, Frik took a wide path that ran alongside vast fields. Magnificent sheaves of tall-stemmed, long-sheaved wheat waved in some fields, while *kukurutz*, the maize of that country, was planted in others. The path led to the edge of a forest of pine and fir trees, cool and dark. Lower down, the Sil went its luminous way, filtered by the gravel in the riverbed; logs cut by the sawmills upstream bobbed on its surface.

Dogs and sheep stopped on the right bank of the river and began drinking greedily, moving aside the tangle of reeds.

Werst wasn't much more than a stone's throw away, beyond a thick plantation of willows, formed by real trees and not those scraggy tadpoles that suffocate a few feet above their roots. This willow plantation continued on to the slopes of the Vulkan Pass; the village that bears this name occupies a projection on the southern slope of the massifs of the Plesa.

The countryside was deserted at that hour. It is only as night falls that people of the fields return to their homes, and Frik was unable to exchange a traditional greeting as he made his way back. Now that his herd had slaked its thirst, he was about to make for the folds of the valley when a man appeared at a bend in the Sil, about fifty feet downstream.

"Hey there, friend!" he shouted to the shepherd.

He was one of those merchants that travel from market to market in the region. They can be found in towns, in hamlets, even in the most humble of villages. They have no trouble making themselves understood: they speak all languages. Was this one Italian, Saxon, or Wallachian? No one could have said; but he was Jewish, a Polish Jew, tall, thin, with a hooked nose, a pointy beard, domed forehead, eyes very lively.

This peddler sold eyeglasses, thermometers, barometers, and little clocks. Whatever wasn't enclosed in the pack fastened to his shoulders with strong straps, hung from his neck and belt: he was a real hawker, something like a walking stall.

Probably this Jew felt the respect, and perhaps the salutary fear, inspired by shepherds. Thus he saluted Frik with his hand. Then, in that Romanian language, which is formed from Latin and Slavic, he said, with a foreign accent:

"Is all well with you, my friend?"

"Yes... depending on the weather," Frik replied.

"So you're well today, then, since it's nice out."

"And I'll be ill tomorrow, since it will rain."

"It will rain?" the peddler cried out. "It can rain without clouds in your country, then?"

"The clouds will come tonight... from over there... from the bad side of the mountain."

"What tells you that?"

"The wool of my sheep, which is rough and dry as tanned leather."

"Then it'll be all the worse for the people traveling on the main roads...."

"And all the better for the ones who've stayed behind the doors of their houses."

"But for that you need to own a house, shepherd."

"Do you have children?" asked Frik.

"No."

"Are you married?"

"No."

And Frik asked that because, in his country, it is the custom to ask this of those one meets.

Then, he went on:

"Where do you come from, peddler?"

"From Hermanstadt."

Hermanstadt is one of the main towns in Transylvania. Leaving it, you come to the Hungarian valley of the Sil, which descends to the hamlet of Petrosani.

"And you are going...?"

"To Kolosvar."

To get to Kolosvar, you have to climb back up in the direction of the Maros valley; then, by Karlsburg, following the first strata of the Bihar mountains, you reach the capital of the district. A road about twenty miles long at most.

In truth, these merchants of thermometers, barometers, and old watches always conjure up the idea of beings set apart, with an allure out of E.T.A. Hoffman. That stems from their livelihood. They sell time and weather in all its forms—time that passes, temperature as it is now, or as it will be, as other merchants sell baskets, wool, or cotton. You could say they are the traveling salesmen of Saturn and Co. under the sign of the Golden Hourglass. And this was surely the effect the Jew had on Frik, who looked, not without surprise, at this display of objects, all new to him, whose purpose he did not know.

"Hey, peddler," he said as he stretched out his arm, "what's all that junk for, clinking on your belt like bones on an old hangman?"

"Those are valuable things," the merchant replied, "things that are useful for everyone."

"For everyone," Frik cried out, "—even shepherds?"

"Even shepherds."

"What about this device...?"

"This device," the Jew replied as he made a thermometer appear between his hands, "tells you if it's warm or cold outside."

"Well, my friend, I can tell that by whether I'm sweating under my tunic, or shivering under my greatcoat."

Obviously, that must have sufficed for a shepherd, who was scarcely concerned with the whys of science.

"And this big old watch with its needle?" he went on, pointing out an aneroid barometer.

"That's not a watch at all, but an instrument that tells you if it will be nice out tomorrow or if it will rain."

"Really?"

"Really."

"Fine!" Frik replied, "I wouldn't want it, even if just cost a kreutzer. Just by seeing the clouds trailing over the mountain or flowing over the highest peaks, don't I know the weather twenty-four hours in advance? Look, see that mist that seems to be rising up from the ground? Well, as I told you before, that'll be tomorrow's water."

In truth, the shepherd Frik, a great observer of weather, could do without a barometer.

"I guess I don't need to ask you if you need a watch," the peddler continued.

"A watch? I have one that works all by itself, and that balances itself over my head. It's the sun up there. See, my friend, when it pauses over the tip of the Roduk, that's because it's noon, and when it peeks through the hole of Egelt, it's six o'clock. My sheep know that as well as I do, my dogs as well as my sheep. Keep your old watches, then."

"Well then," the peddler replied, "if shepherds were my only customers, I'd have trouble making a living! You don't need anything, then...?"

"Not even anything."

What's more, all this low-priced merchandise was of very poor workmanship; the barometers disagreed with each other, some predicting "change," others "steady"; the hour hands were slow or the minute hands fast —in fact it was all pure rubbish. Perhaps the shepherd suspected this, and was hardly inclined to present himself as a buyer. Still, just as he was about to pick up his crook, he spun round a kind of tube, hung from the peddler's strap, and said:

"What's the use of this tube you have here?"

"This tube isn't a tube."

"Is it a muzzle loader, then?"

And the shepherd meant by this a kind of old pistol with a flared barrel.

"No," said the Jew, "it's a spyglass."

It was one of those common telescopes, which magnify objects five to six times, or make them seem five or six times closer, which produces the same result.

Frik had detached the instrument; he looked at it, handled it, turned it round and round, made its cylinders slide over each other.

Then, shaking his head, he said, "A spyglass?"

"Yes, shepherd, a first-rate one too, that lengthens your sight very nicely."

"Oh! I have good eyes, my friend. When the weather's clear, I can see the last rocks up to the head of Retyezat, and the last trees at the bottom of the Vulkan gorges."

"Without blinking?"

"Without blinking. It's the dew that does that for me, when I sleep out in the open at night. That cleans your eyes just right."

"What—the dew?" the peddler said. "I'd think it would make you blind, rather...."

"Not shepherds."

"Maybe! But if you have good eyes, mine are even better, when I put them to the tip of my spyglass."

"That remains to be seen."

"See for yourself, by putting your own eyes to it."

"Me?"

"Try it."

"It won't cost me anything?" asked Frik, very mistrustful by nature.

"Nothing... unless you decide to buy the mechanism from me."

Reassured in this regard, Frik took the spyglass, whose tubes were adjusted by the peddler. Then, having closed his left eye, he applied the eyepiece to his right eye.

First of all, he looked in the direction of the Vulkan Pass, then up to the Plesa. That done, he lowered the instrument, and aimed it at the village of Werst.

"Well, well! It's true.... It carries farther than my eyes.... There's the main street.... I can recognize the people.... Look, there's Nic Deck, the forester, returning from his round, with his knapsack on his back, his rifle on his shoulder...."

"Just as I told you!" the peddler observed.

"Yes... yes... it's really Nic!" the shepherd continued. "And who's the girl coming out of the house of Master Koltz, in a red skirt and black blouse, making as if to go in front of him?"

"Look, shepherd, you'll recognize the girl as well as the boy...."

"Oh, yes! It's Miriota... beautiful Miriota! Ah! Lovers... lovers! This time, they'll have to behave, since I have them at the tip of my tube, and I won't miss one of their little quirks!"

"What do you think of my machine?"

"Nice, nice! How far it lets you see!"

For Frik never to have looked through a spyglass before, the village of Werst had to have been ranked among the most backward in the district of Klausenburg. And it was, as we'll soon see.

"Come then, shepherd," the merchant went on, "aim at something else... further away than Werst.... The village is too close to us. Aim beyond it, well beyond it, I tell you!"

"And that won't cost me any more?"

"No more."

"Good! I'll look on the side of the Hungarian Sil! Yes... there's the belltower of Livadzel.... I recognize it from its cross, which is missing an arm.... And, beyond it, in the valley, between the fir trees, I can see the belltower of Petrosani, with its tin rooster, whose beak is open, as if he were going to call his hens! And there, that tower that points up from the midst of the trees.... That must be the tower of Petrilla.... But, now that I think of it, peddler, wait a bit, since it's still the same price...."

"Still the same, shepherd."

Frik had just turned around towards the Plateau of Orgall; then, from the end of the telescope, he followed the curtain of darkened forests over the slopes of the Plesa, and the lens framed the distant outline of the castle.

"Yes!" he cried, "the fourth branch is on the ground.... I did see right! And no one will go gather it to make a nice torch for Saint John.... No, no one... not even me! That would be risking body and soul.... But don't bother yourself! There is someone who can shove it, tonight, into the midst of his hellfire.... That's the Chort!"

"The Chort"—the Black One—is what the devil is called, when he is mentioned in countryside conversations.

Perhaps the Jew was about to ask for an explanation

of these words, incomprehensible for anyone not from the village of Werst or its environs, but then Frik cried out, in a voice in which terror was mingled with surprise:

"What is that, that mist escaping from the castle keep? Is it a mist? No! It looks like smoke.... It's not possible! For years and years, the chimneys of the castle have stopped smoking!"

"If you see smoke there, shepherd, that's because there is smoke."

"No, peddler, no! It's the glass in your machine that's fogging up."

"Wipe it."

"And after I wipe it?"

Frik turned the telescope around, and, after rubbing the lens with his sleeve, put it back to his eye.

It was indeed smoke that was pouring from the tip of the castle keep. It rose straight up into the calm air, and its plume mixed with the high haze.

Frik, motionless, stopped speaking. All his attention was concentrated on the castle, on which the increasing darkness was beginning to encroach, reaching the level of the Plateau of Orgall.

Suddenly he lowered the spyglass, and, reaching for the pouch that hung beneath his tunic:

"How much is your tube?" he asked.

"A florin and a half," the peddler replied.

And he would have yielded his spyglass for even one florin, if Frik had shown any inclination to bargain for it. But the shepherd didn't turn a hair. Visibly under the power of an amazement as sudden as it was inexplicable, he plunged his hand to the bottom of his pouch and took some money out of it.

"Are you buying this spyglass for yourself?" asked the peddler.

"No... for my master, Judge Koltz."

"Then he'll reimburse you...."

"Yes... the two florins it cost me...."

"What do you mean? Two florins?"

"Yes indeed! There you are. Goodnight, my friend."

"Good night, shepherd."

And Frik, whistling for his dogs, urging on his herd, quickly climbed up in the direction of Werst.

The Jew, watching him without moving, shook his head, as if he had been dealing with some kind of madman:

"If I'd have known," he murmured, "I'd have sold it dearer, my spyglass!"

Then, when he had readjusted his display on his belt and on his shoulders, he took the direction of Karlsburg, going down the right bank of the Sil.

Where was he going? It doesn't matter. He is only passing through this tale. We won't see him again.

I I

Whether it's a matter of rocks piled up by nature during geologic eras after the final convulsions of the earth, or of buildings constructed by man over which the breath of time has passed, the aspect is pretty much the same, when you observe them from a few miles distant. Unworked stone and wrought stone are all easily confused. From a distance, they're the same color, they have the same outlines, the same deviations of lines in perspective, the same uniformity of tint beneath the grayish patina of the centuries.

Thus it was with the citadel—that is, the castle—in the Carpathians. To recognize the vague shapes on this Plateau of Orgall, which the castle crowns on the left side of the Vulkan Pass, would not have been possible. It does not stand out against the background of the mountains. What one is tempted to take for a keep might perhaps be just a stony hill. Whoever looks at it thinks he sees the crenellations of a fortified wall, where there might be nothing but a rocky crest. It is all vague, floating, uncertain. Thus, if one is to believe various tourists, the Castle of the Carpathians exists only in the imagination of the people in the district.

Obviously, the simplest way to make sure would be to hire a guide from Vulkan or Werst, climb the gorge, mount the hilltop, and visit the totality of these constructions. Only it's even harder to find a guide than it is to find the path that leads to the citadel. In this country of the two Sils, no one would agree to lead a traveler, no matter the remuneration, to this Castle of the Carpathians.

Whatever may be the case, here is what you could have seen of this ancient abode in the viewfinder of a telescope, one more powerful and better focused than the cheap instrument bought by the shepherd Frik on behalf of Master Koltz: Set back 800 or 900 feet from the Vulkan Pass, a battlement, color of sandstone, covered with a jumble of lapidary plants, extending to a periphery of about 2,500 to 3,000 feet around, conforming to the unevenness of the plateau; at each end, two corner bastions; the bastion on the right, on which the famous beech tree grew, is also surmounted by a slender watchtower or sentry box with a pointed roof; on the left, a few sections of wall are supported by openwork buttresses, which prop up the belltower of a chapel, whose cracked bell is set swinging by strong gusts of wind, to the great terror of the country folk; in the middle, finally, crowned by its crenellated terreplein, is a ponderous castle keep, with three rows of leaded windows, the first floor of which is surrounded by a circular terrace; on the terre-plein is a long metal shaft embellished with the feudal virolet, a kind of weathervane fused in place by rust, which a final blast of wind had fixed pointing to the southeast.

As to what this wall, broken in many places, was encircling, or whether there still existed some building that was inhabitable within, or whether a drawbridge and barbican allowed one to enter it, people had ceased to know for a number of years. Actually, although the Castle of the Carpathians was better preserved than it looked, a contagious horror, increased by superstition, protected it just as much as its basilisks, its catapults, its bombards, its culverins, its thunderers, and other artillery mechanisms would have done in the old days.

And yet, the Castle of the Carpathians would have been worth the trouble of a visit from tourists and antiquarians. Its situation, on the top of the Plateau of Orgall, is exceptionally beautiful. From the upper terreplein of the keep, the view extends out to the extreme limit of the mountains. In the background undulates the lofty mountain chain, so capriciously ramified, that marks the border with Wallachia. In front, the sinuous gorge of the Vulkan is hollowed out, the only navigable road between the adjoining provinces. Beyond the valley of the two Sils, the hamlets of Livadzel, Lonyai, Petrosani, and Petrilla appear, grouped around the openings of mineshafts that serve to exploit this rich coal-bearing area. Then, in the far distance, there is an admirable thrust fault of mountains, wooded at their bases, lush with greenery at their sides, arid at their summits, dominated by the sharp summits of the Retyezat and Paring mountains.* Finally, farther away than the Hatszeg valley and the Maros river, the distant outlines, drowned in mist, of the Alps of Central Transylvania appear.

At the bottom of this crater, the subsiding of the ground long ago formed a lake in which the two Sils were absorbed, before they found their way through the chain of mountains. Now, though, this depression is nothing more than a coalmine, with its inconveniences and its advantages; high brick chimneys mingle with the boughs of poplar, fir, and beech trees; black smoke pollutes the air, which had before been saturated with the smell of fruit trees and flowers. Still, at the time this story occurs, although industry holds this mining district under its iron hand, it has lost none of the wild qualities it owes to nature.

The Castle of the Carpathians dates back to the twelfth or thirteenth century. In that time, under the domination of war chiefs or *voivods*, the monasteries, churches, palaces, and castles were fortified with as much care as the hamlets or villages. Lords and peasants had to secure themselves against aggression of all kinds. This state of things explains why the ancient walled fortification of the castle, its bastions and its keep, give it the look of a feudal construction, intended for defense. What architect built it on this plateau, at this height? We do not know, and that bold artist remains anonymous, unless he is the Romanian master mason Manole, so gloriously sung of in the Wallachian legends, who built the famous Monastery of Curtea de Arges for Neagoe Basarab, the Black Prince.

If there is uncertainty about the architect, there is none about the family that owned this castle. The Barons

* The Retyezat rises up to a height of 8,189 feet, and the Paring to a height 7,920 feet above sea level.

of Gortz had been lords in the country from time immemorial. They were involved in all those wars that blood-
ied the Transylvanian provinces; they fought against the
Hungarians, the Saxons, the Szekelers; their name figures in those folk ballads and chronicles called *cantices*
and *doïnas*, where the memory of these disastrous periods
is perpetuated; their motto was the famous Wallachian
proverb: *Da pe maorte*!, "Give until death!", and they
gave, and spilled their blood for the cause of independence—the blood that came to them from the Romanians,
their ancestors.

As we know, all those efforts, devotion, and sacrifices
led only to reducing the descendants of this valiant race
to the most shameful oppression. It no longer has any
political existence. Three heels have crushed it. But they
do not despair of shaking off the yoke, these Wallachians
of Transylvania. The future belongs to them, and it is
with an unwavering confidence they repeat these words,
in which all their aspirations are concentrated: *Rôman on
péré*!, "The Romanian cannot perish!"

Around the middle of the nineteenth century, the last
representative of the Lords of Gortz was the Baron
Rudolf. Born in the Castle of the Carpathians, he had
seen his family die around him during his early youth. At
the age of 22, he found himself alone in the world. All his
people had fallen from one year to the next, like those
branches of the age-old beech tree, with which popular
superstition connected the very existence of the castle.
Without parents, one can even say without friends, what
would Baron Rudolf do to pass the time in this monoto-
nous solitude that death had created around him? What
were his tastes, his instincts, his aptitudes? One could

scarcely say, unless it's an irresistible passion for music, especially for the singing of the great artists of that era. So one day, abandoning the castle, already greatly dilapidated, to the care of a few old servants, he disappeared. It was learned later on that he devoted his fortune, which was rather considerable, to traveling through the principal lyric centers of Europe, the theaters of Germany, France, and Italy, where he could satisfy his insatiable dilettante whims. Was he an eccentric, if not a maniac? The oddness of his existence gave one reason to believe so.

However, the memory of the country had remained profoundly engraved in the heart of the young Baron Gortz. He had not forgotten his Transylvanian homeland in the course of his distant peregrinations. Thus he returned to take part in one of the bloody revolts of the Romanian peasants against Hungarian oppression.

The descendants of the ancient Dacians were conquered, and their territory fell to the conquerors, to be divided up.

It was after this defeat that Baron Rudolf left the Castle of the Carpathians once and for all, some parts of which had already fallen in ruin. Death wasn't slow to deprive the castle of its last servants, and it was completely abandoned. As for Baron Gortz, rumor had it that he had patriotically joined up with the famous Sandor Rosza, a former highway robber, whom the war for independence had made a tragic hero. Fortunately for him, after the battle, Rudolf of Gortz had separated from the band of the compromising *betyar*, and he acted wisely, since the former brigand, who had once again become a leader of thieves, ended up falling into the hands of the police, who were content with locking him up in the prison of Szamos-Uyvar.

Nonetheless, one version was generally believed among the people of the district: namely that Baron Rudolf had been killed during a confrontation between Sandor Rosza and customs officers at the border. This wasn't the least bit true, although Baron Gortz had never shown himself again at the castle since that time, and no one doubted his death. But it is prudent to accept the hearsay of this credulous population with caution.

Abandoned castle, haunted castle, vision-filled castle. The lively, ardent imaginings of the people soon populated it with ghosts; the walking dead appeared there, spirits returned there during the night hours. That is how things still occur in the heart of certain superstitious countries of Europe, and Transylvania can claim first place among them.

What's more, how could this village of Werst abandon belief in the supernatural? The priest and the schoolmaster—one guiding the religion of the faithful, the other in charge of educating the children—taught these fables all the more openly since they truly believed them. They asserted, "with proofs to back them up," that werewolves ran through the countryside, that vampires, called *stryges* because they let out the cries of owls, quenched their thirst on human blood, that the *staffi* wander among the ruins and become evil, if one forgets to bring them something to drink and eat every night. There are fairies, *babes*, which one must be careful not to meet on Tuesday or Friday, the two most evil days of the week. Venture, then, into the depths of those forests of the district, enchanted forests, where the *balaurs* are hidden, those giant dragons, whose jaws can stretch up to the clouds, the *zmei* with enormous wings, who kidnap girls of royal blood and even those of lower stock, if they're pretty! That seems like a good number of fearsome monsters; and what is the good genie that popular imagination confronts them with? None other than the *serpi de casa*, the snake of the domestic hearth, who lives familiarly in back of the fireplace, and whose salutary influence the peasant solicits by feeding it with his best milk.

Now, if ever a castle was built to serve as a refuge to the inhabitants of this Romanian mythology, isn't it the Castle of the Carpathians? On that isolated plateau, inaccessible except from the left side of the Vulkan Pass, there was no doubt it sheltered dragons, fairies, *stryges*, perhaps also a few ghosts from the family of the Barons of Gortz. Thence its unsavory reputation, quite justified, people said. As for taking the risk of visiting it, no one would have thought of it. It spread around it a terrible epidemic, just as an insalubrious swamp spreads its pestilential miasma. Just coming within a quarter of a mile of it would be to risk your life in this world and your salvation in the next. This was what was currently being taught at Master Hermod's school.

Still, this state of things had to come to an end, as soon as the last stone of the ancient fortress of the Barons of Gortz fell. And here is where legend played its part.

According to the most authoritative citizens of Werst, the existence of the castle was linked to that of the old beech tree, whose boughs grimaced over the corner bastion, at the right of the battlement wall.

Since the departure of Rudolf of Gortz—the people

of the village, especially the shepherd Frik, had kept an eye on it—every year this beech tree lost one of its principal branches. People counted eighteen branches stemming from its main trunk when Baron Rudolf was seen for the last time on the terreplein of the keep, and the tree now had only three left. And every time a branch fell, a year was subtracted from the castle's existence. The fall of the last branch would bring about its complete annihilation. And then, on the Plateau of Orgall, you would search in vain for the remains of the Castle of the Carpathians.

Actually, that was just one of those legends that readily spring up in the Romanian imagination. And, first of all, did this old beech tree cut off one of its own branches every year? That was in no sense proven, although Frik didn't hesitate to assert it, since he never lost sight of it while his herd was grazing on the pastures of the Sil. Nonetheless, and although Frik was unreliable, for the lowest peasant as well as for the chief magistrate in Werst, there was no doubt that the castle had no more than three years left to live, since there were only three branches left on the "tutelary beech."

So the shepherd was on his way back to the village to bring back this important news, when the incident of the telescope occurred.

Important news, very important in fact! Smoke had appeared at the top of the keep.... What his eyes could not have glimpsed, Frik had distinctly seen with the peddler's instrument.... It's not a mist, it's smoke that's going up and mingling with the clouds.... And yet, the castle is abandoned.... For a very long time no one had passed through its barbican, which is no doubt closed, or

the drawbridge, which is certainly raised. If it is inhabited, it can only be by supernatural beings.... But what
was the intention of the spirits in making a fire in one of
the apartments in the keep? Is it a bedroom fire, or a
cooking fire? That's what's truly inexplicable.

Frik hurried his animals towards their barn.
Following his command, the dogs urged the flock up the
rising path, its dust vying with the evening damp.

Some farmers, having lingered over their fields,
greeted him in passing, and he scarcely replied to their
politeness. This was a source of real anxiety for them,
since, if you want to avoid a curse, it is not enough to say
hello to a shepherd; he has to return the greeting. But
Frik seemed little inclined to do so, with his haggard
eyes, his singular attitude, his disorderly gestures. He
could not have looked more defeated if wolves and bears
had made off with half his sheep. What bad news could
he be the bearer of?

The first one to learn it was Judge Koltz. Far off as he
was, as soon as he saw him Frik cried out to him:

"There is fire in the castle, master!"

"What are you saying, Frik?"

"I am telling the truth."

"Have you gone crazy?"

In fact, how could a fire attack this old pile of stones?
Might as well say that the Negoi, the highest peak of the
Carpathians, was being devoured by flames. That would
not have been more absurd.

"You are claiming, Frik, you are claiming that the castle is burning?" Master Koltz repeated.

"If it isn't burning, it's smoking."

"It's some kind of mist...."

"No, it's smoke.... Come look."

And both of them headed for the middle of the main street of the village, on the edge of a terrace dominating the ravines of the Pass, where you could make out the castle.

Once there, Frik held out the telescope to Master Koltz.

Obviously, the use of this instrument was no more known to him than it had been to the shepherd.

"What is this?" he said.

"A machine I bought for you for two florins, master, which is well worth four!"

"From whom?"

"From a peddler."

"And what for?"

"Adjust that to your eye, aim at the castle opposite, look, and you'll see."

The judge aimed the spyglass in the direction of the castle and examined it for a long time.

Yes! It was smoke that was coming from one of the chimneys in the keep. At that moment, blown by the breeze, it was creeping over the mountainside.

"Smoke!" Master Koltz repeated, stupefied.

However, Frik and he had just been joined by Miriota and the forester Nic Deck, who had just recently returned home.

"What's this for?" the young man asked, taking the spyglass.

"To see far away," the shepherd replied.

"Are you joking, Frik?"

"I joke so little, forester, that scarcely an hour ago, I was able to recognize you, as you were coming down the road to Werst, you and also...."

He didn't finish his sentence. Miriota had blushed, lowering her pretty eyes. In fact, though, it is not forbidden for an honest girl to walk in front of her fiancé.

Both of them, one after the other, took the famous spyglass and directed it at the castle.

In the meantime, half a dozen neighbors had arrived on the terrace, and, having learned how, they each used the instrument in turn.

"Smoke! Smoke in the castle!" said one.

"Maybe lightning has struck the keep?" another observed.

"Has there been any lightning?" Master Koltz asked Frik.

"Not one bolt in eight days," the shepherd replied.

And these brave people would not have been more astonished if they had been told that the mouth of a crater had just opened up at the summit of Mt. Retyezat, and was emitting subterranean vapors.

III

The village of Werst has so little importance that most maps don't even indicate its location. In the administrative system, it is even beneath its neighbor, called Vulkan, from the name of that portion of the Plesa massif on which they are both picturesquely perched.

At the present time, the exploitation of the mining basin has brought a considerable amount of commerce to the hamlets of Petrosani, Livadzel and others, a few miles distant. Neither Vulkan nor Werst received the least advantage from this proximity to a major industrial center; what these villages were fifty years ago, what they undoubtedly will be in half a century, they are at present; and, according to Elisée Reclus, a good half of the population of Vulkan is made up solely of "employees in charge of keeping watch over the border, customs officers, policemen, tax clerks and medical attendants in the quarantine center." Take away the policemen and tax clerks, add a slightly larger number of farmers, and you'll have the population of Werst, about four to five hundred inhabitants.

This village is a street—nothing but a wide street, whose sharp inclines make its ascent and descent somewhat difficult. It serves as a natural route between the Wallachian and Transylvanian borders. Herds of cattle, sheep, and pigs pass by; sellers of fresh meat, fruits, and grains; and rare travelers who venture into the gorge, instead of taking the railways of Kolosvar and the valley of the Maros.

Indeed, nature has generously endowed this basin hollowed out between the mountains of Bihar, Reyezat, and Paring. Rich from the fertility of the soil, it is also rich with all the wealth hidden away in its bowels: rock salt mines in Thorda, with an annual yield of more than twenty thousand tons; Mount Parajd, measuring seven kilometers in circumference at its dome, and composed solely of sodium chloride; the mines of Torotzko, which produce lead, galenite, mercury, and especially iron, whose deposits were exploited as early as the tenth century; the mines of Vayda Hunyad, and their iron ore, which is transformed into steel of superior quality; coal mines, easily workable on the first strata of these lakeside valleys, in the district of Hatszeg, in Livadzel, in Petrosani, vast pockets of a yield estimated at 250 million tons; gold mines, finally, in the hamlet of Offenbanya, in Topanfalva, the region of the gold sifters, where myriads of mills of very simple construction process the sands of Veres-Patak, "the Transylvanian Pactolus," the river of gold, and every year export two million francs' worth of precious metal.

Here, it seems, is a district very well favored by nature, and yet this wealth scarcely improves the well-being of its population. In any case, though the most important centers—Torotzko, Petrosani, Lonyai—have some installations in keeping with the comfort of modern industry, though these hamlets have conventional constructions, subject to the uniformity of the T-square and plumb-line, warehouses, stores, veritable workers' cities, though they are endowed with a certain number of dwellings with balconies and verandas, there's no use looking for these things in either the village of Vulkan, or the village of Werst.

A careful count finds about sixty houses, irregularly crouching by the side of the single street, each topped with a capricious roof whose eaves overlap the stucco walls, the front facing the garden, a loft with a skylight as its sole upper floor, a dilapidated barn as an annex, a lop-sided cowshed covered with mulch, here and there a well surmounted by a bracket from which a bucket is hanging, two or three ponds that "leak" during storms, some streams whose twisting ruts indicate their course: such is the village of Werst, built on both sides of the street, between the steep embankments of the pass. But all this is fresh and attractive; there are flowers in the doorways and at the windows, curtains of greenery covering the walls, wild grasses that mingle with the old gold of the stubble fields, poplars, elms, beech trees, firs, maple trees, that rise above the houses "as high as they can climb." Beyond, the intermediary strata of the foothills spread out, and, far off, the last summits of the mountain chain, turned blue by distance, mingle with the azure of the sky.

They speak neither German nor Hungarian in Werst, or in that whole portion of Transylvania: it's Romanian they speak—even among some Gypsy families, more settled than camping in the various villages of the district. These foreigners adopt the language of the country just as they adopt its religion. The ones in Werst form a kind of little clan under the authority of a *voivode*, with their caravans, their "barakas" with pointed roofs, their legions of children, very different in their customs and the regularity of their existence from those of their fellows who wander throughout Europe. They even follow the Greek Orthodox rituals, adapting themselves to the religion of the Christians in the midst of whom they have settled. In fact, Werst has an Orthodox priest as its religious head, who resides in Vulkan, and who serves both villages, which are separated by only half a mile.

Civilization is like air or water. Wherever a passage—even if it's just a fissure—is opened to it, it penetrates and modifies the conditions of a country. However, it should be acknowledged that no fissure had yet been produced throughout this southern portion of the Carpathians. Since Elisée Reclus could say that Vulkan "is the last outpost of civilization in the valley of the Wallachian Sil," you will not be surprised that Werst was one of the most backward villages of the district of Kolosvar. How could it be otherwise in these places where everyone is born, grows up, and dies, without ever leaving them!

And yet, someone will point out, isn't there a schoolmaster, and a judge, in Werst? Yes, of course. But Master Hermod is capable of teaching only what he knows, that is to say a little reading, a little writing, a little counting. His personal instruction does not go beyond that. In matters of science, history, geography, literature, he knows only the popular songs and legends of the surrounding countryside. On that subject, his memory serves him with a rare abundance. He is very strong in whatever deals with the fantastic, and the few schoolboys in the village draw great benefit from his lessons.

As for the judge, we should clarify this title given to the main magistrate of Werst.

The *biró*, Master Koltz, was a little man about 55 or 60 years old, Romanian in origin, hair sparse and graying, moustache still black, eyes more gentle than keen. Solidly built like a mountain dweller, he wore a vast felt hat on his head, a high belt with a historiated buckle on his stomach, a sleeveless vest on his torso, short, half-baggy trousers tucked into tall leather boots. More a mayor than a judge, although his functions obliged him to intervene in various difficulties between neighbors, his main occupation was administering his village authoritatively and not without some amenity for his purse. In fact, all transactions, purchases or sales, were subject to a tax to his advantage—not to mention the toll tax that foreigners, tourists, or merchants hurried to pour into his pocket.

This lucrative situation had brought a certain affluence to Master Koltz. If most of the peasants of the district are worn away by usury, which soon makes Israelite money-lenders the real owners of the soil, the *biró* had been able to escape their rapaciousness. His property, free from mortgages, or "intabulations" as they say in this country, owed nothing to no one. He would rather

lend than borrow, and would certainly have done so without fleecing the poor populace. He owned several pastures, good grazing ground for his herds; cultivated fields
decently maintained, although he was resistant to new
methods; vineyards that flattered his vanity when he
strolled alongside the vines loaded with clusters of
grapes, whose harvest he sold profitably—with the
exception, and that is of a considerable size, of what his
own consumption required.

It goes without saying that Master Koltz's house is
the finest house in the village, at the corner of the terrace
that the long climbing street crosses. A house made of
stone, if you please, with its front facing the garden, its
door between the third and fourth window, the festoons
of greenery that hem the gutter with their budding twigs,
the two tall beech trees branching out over his flowering
thatch. Behind, a beautiful orchard lines up its vegetable
plants in a grid, and its rows of fruit trees overflow onto
the talus of the pass. Inside the house, there are fine,
very clean rooms, some to eat in, others to sleep in with
their paint-daubed furniture, tables, beds, benches and
stools, their hutches where pots and plates gleam, the
exposed beams of the ceiling, from which ribboned vases
hang and brightly colored fabric, the heavy chests, which
serve as sideboards and cupboards, covered with quilts
and counterpanes; then, on the white walls, the violent-
ly colored portraits of Romanian patriots—among others,
the popular fifteenth-century hero, the *voivode* Vayda-
Hunyad.

A charming habitation, which would have been too
big for one man alone. But he was not alone, our Master
Koltz. Widowed for a dozen years, he had a daughter, the

beautiful Miriota, much admired from Werst to Vulkan and even beyond. She could have had one of those strange pagan names like Florica, Daina, Dauritia, which are highly favored among Wallachian families. No! hers was Miriota, or "little ewe." But she had grown up, the little ewe. She was now a graceful girl of 20 years, blonde with brown eyes, a very sweet gaze, charming in her features, pleasant bearing. Actually, there were some serious reasons for her to seem even more seductive, with her blouse embroidered with red thread at the neck, wrists, and shoulders, her skirt drawn in with a silver clasp, her "catrinza," a full-length pinafore with blue and red stripes, tied at her waist, her little boots of yellow leather, the light kerchief thrown over her head, her long hair waving, plaits adorned with a ribbon or a small metal coin.

Yes! She is a beautiful girl, Miriota Koltz, and—which doesn't spoil anything—rich for this village lost deep in the Carpathians. Good housekeeper? Undoubtedly, since she cleverly keeps her father's house in order. Well-taught? Indeed yes! At Master Hermod's school, she learned how to read, write, calculate; and she calculates, writes, and reads correctly, but she was pushed no further—and with good reason. On the other hand, no one could teach her anything more about Transylvanian fables and sagas. She knows as much as her teacher. She knows the legend of Leany-Ko, the Rock of the Virgin, where a young rather fantastic princess escapes the pursuits of the Tartars; the legend of the Dragon's cave, in the valley of the "Ascent of the King"; the legend of the Deva fortress, which was built "in the time of the Fairies"; the legend of the Detunata, the one "Struck by

Thunder," that famous basalt mountain, like unto a giant stone violin, on which the devil plays during stormy nights; the legend of the Retyezat with its summit razed by a sorcerer; the legend of the gorge of Thorda, split with one great blow by the sword of Saint Ladislas. We will confess that Miriota had faith in all these fictions, but she was no less charming and likeable a girl.

Many boys throughout the countryside found her to their liking, even without reminding themselves too much that she was the sole heir of the *biró*, Master Koltz, the leading magistrate in Werst. However it was useless to court her. Wasn't she already engaged to Nicolas Deck?

A fine specimen of a Romanian was this Nicolas or rather Nic Deck: 25 years old, tall of stature, vigorous constitution, head held proudly erect, black hair covered by the white kolpak, honest gaze, casual manner in his lambskin jacket embroidered at the seams. He stood firmly planted on his slim legs, the legs of a stag, and he showed resolution in his gait and his gestures. He was a forester by trade, which means he was almost as much a soldier as he was a civilian. Since he owned some cultivated fields in the environs of Werst, he pleased her father, and since he presented himself as a likeable boy of proud bearing, he didn't at all displease the girl, for whom he would brook no rivals—he wouldn't even allow anyone else to look at her too closely. But no one thought of doing so.

The wedding of Nic Deck and Miriota Koltz was to be celebrated in a few weeks, around the middle of the next month. The village would deck itself out for a big celebration then. Master Koltz would arrange things admirably. He wasn't the least bit greedy. Though he liked earning money, he didn't refuse to spend it on occasion. Then, once the ceremony was completed, Nic Deck would take up residence in the family house, which would be passed on to him by the *biró*, and when Miriota felt him close to her, she would no longer be afraid, when she heard a door groaning or the furniture creaking during the long winter nights, of seeing the apparition of some ghost escaped from her favorite legends.

To complete the list of the noteworthy people of Werst, two more should be cited, no less important: the schoolmaster and the doctor.

Schoolmaster Hermod was a fat man with glasses, 55 years of age, always holding the curved bit of his pipe clenched in his teeth, the pipe with a porcelain bowl. He had sparse, disheveled hair on a flat skull; a clean-shaven face with a tic in his left cheek. His main concern was trimming the quill pens of his students, whom he forbade from using steel pens—on the principle of the thing. How many nibs he lengthened, with his well-sharpened old penknife! With what precision, screwing up his eyes, did he give the final flourish to slice its tip! Beautiful handwriting came before everything else; that was what all his efforts were for, that is what a master anxious to fulfill his mission strove to make his students realize. Teaching came second—and we know what Schoolmaster Hermod taught, what the generations of boys and girls learned on the benches of his school!

And now for Dr. Patak.

What's that, there was a doctor in Werst, and the village still believed in the supernatural?

Yes, but you have to understand the meaning of the title that Dr. Patak took, as we had to understand the title used by Judge Koltz.

Patak was a little man with a prominent embonpoint, fat and short, 45 years of age, very conspicuously practicing standard medicine in Werst and its environs. With his imperturbable aplomb and his deafening loquaciousness, he inspired no less confidence than the shepherd Frik—which is saying a lot. He sold consultations and drugs, but such inoffensive ones that they only prevented his patients' scrapes from getting worse; they would have gotten better on their own. Moreover, the people of the Vulkan Pass are generally healthy; the air there is of the best quality, epidemic illnesses are unknown, and if you die, it's because everyone has to die, even in this privileged corner of Transylvania. As to Dr. Patak—yes! They called him "doctor"—and although he was accepted as one, he had had no training—not in medicine, not in dispensing drugs, not in anything. He was simply a former quarantine attendant, whose role consisted of watching over the travelers held back on the border for reasons of health. Nothing more. That, it seems, was enough for the undemanding population of Werst. It should be added—which shouldn't surprise anyone—that Dr. Patak was a freethinker, as is only right for whoever takes care of looking after his fellows. Further, he didn't acknowledge any of the superstitions that were rampant in the region of the Carpathians, not even the ones concerning the castle. He laughed about them, joked about them. And, when someone said to him that no one had dared approach the castle since time immemorial: "Why don't you challenge me to go visit your old hut?" he would say to anyone who would listen.

But, since no one challenged him to do so, since everyone even took care not to challenge him, Dr. Patak had never gone there and, with the help of credulity, the Castle in the Carpathians continued to be enveloped in impenetrable mystery.

IV

In a few minutes, the news reported by the shepherd had spread throughout the village. Master Koltz, with the precious telescope in hand, had just gone back to his house, followed by Nic Deck and Miriota. At that moment, the only people remaining on the terrace were Frik, surrounded by twenty or so men, women, and children, who had been joined by some Gypsies, who were by no means the least excited of the Werst population. Frik was surrounded and questioned; the shepherd replied with that haughty importance of a man who had just seen something entirely extraordinary.

"Yes!" he repeated, "the castle was smoking, it's still smoking, and it will keep smoking as long as there's still stone on stone!"

"But who could have lit that fire?" an old woman asked, clasping her hands.

"The *Chort*," Frik answered, giving the devil the name he had in this country, "and he's the crafty one who knows more about keeping fires going than putting them out!"

And, at this reply, everyone began trying to see the smoke at the tip of the keep. In the end, most of them asserted they could see it perfectly, although it was perfectly invisible at that distance.

The effect produced by this singular phenomenon surpassed everything anyone could imagine. It is necessary to insist on this point. If the reader is willing to put himself in a state of mind identical to that of the people of Werst, he will not be at all surprised at the facts that will be related later on. I am not asking him to believe in the supernatural, but to remember that this ignorant population believed in it without reservation. The mistrust the Castle of the Carpathians inspired when people took it to be deserted was soon to be joined by terror, since it seemed inhabited—and by what kinds of beings, great God!

There was a meeting-place in Werst, frequented by drinkers, and even favored by those who, without drinking, like to talk about their affairs, when the day is done—the latter group in rather limited numbers, it goes without saying. This place, which was open to everyone, was the main, or rather, the only inn in the village.

Who was the proprietor of this inn? A Jew by the name of Jonas, a fine fellow of about 60 years of age, with an engaging but very Semitic physiognomy, with his black eyes, curved nose, protruding lip, flat hair and the traditional chinbeard. Obsequious and obliging, he readily lent small sums of money to one person or another, without being too demanding about the securities, or too much of a usurer for the interest, although it was understood he would be paid on the date agreed to by the borrower. If only all the Jews settled in the Transylvanian country were always as accommodating as the innkeeper at Werst!

Unfortunately, this excellent Jonas is an exception. His fellow worshippers in his faith, his colleagues in the profession—for they are all innkeepers, selling drinks and foodstuffs—practice the profession of lender with a fierceness that is worrisome for the future of the Romanian peasant. Little by little the land will pass from the native race to the foreign one. When their loans are not repaid, the Jews will become owners of fine cultivated land mortgaged to their profit, and if the Promised Land is no longer in Judea, it might figure one day on the maps of Transylvanian geography.

The King Mathias Inn—such was its name—occupied one of the corners of the terrace crossed by the main street of Werst, opposite the house of the *biró*. It was an old building, half wood, half stone, well-patched in some places, generally draped with greenery, quite alluring in its appearance. It consisted of only a ground floor, with a glass door opening onto the terrace. Inside, you came first to a large room, furnished with tables for the glasses and stools for the drinkers, a dresser of worm-eaten oak, where the plates, pots, and mugs shone, and a bar of blackened wood, behind which Jonas catered to his clientele.

Now a description of how this room received daylight: two windows were set into the façade, on the terrace, and there were two other windows, opposite, in the back wall. Of these two, one of them, veiled by a thick curtain of climbing or hanging plants that screened the outside, was blocked, and let only a little light in. The other, when you opened it, allowed the astonished gaze to encompass the entire lower valley of the Vulkan. A few feet below the embrasure flowed the turbulent waters of the Nyad river. On one side, the river came down from the hillsides of the pass, after taking its source from the summits of the Plateau of Orgall, crowned by the masonry of the castle; on the other, always abundantly supplied by the streams from the mountain, even during the summer, it hurtled roaring down to the bed of the Wallachian Sil, which absorbed it as it went along.

On the right, adjacent to the main room, half a dozen little bedrooms sufficed to lodge the rare travelers who, before crossing the border, wanted to rest at the King Mathias. They were assured of a warm welcome and moderate prices from an attentive, helpful host, always well-stocked with good tobacco that he found at the best "trafiks" in the environs. As to him, Jonas, his bedroom was a narrow attic, whose oddly shaped skylight, piercing the flowering thatch, looked out onto the terrace.

It was in this inn that, on that very evening of May 29th, there was a meeting of the leading personages of Werst: Master Koltz, Magister Hermod, the forester Nic Deck, a dozen of the principal inhabitants of the village, and also the shepherd Frik, who was not the least important of these characters. Dr. Patak was missing from this meeting of noteworthy men. Asked in all haste by one of his old patients who was only waiting to see him before he passed into the other world, he had agreed to come as soon as his ministrations were no longer indispensable to the deceased.

As they waited for the ex-attendant, they discussed the grave event of the day, but they didn't talk without eating and drinking. To some, Jonas offered that kind of gruel or pudding made from cornmeal, known by the name of "mamaliga," which is not at all unpleasant when you ingest it with freshly drawn milk. To others, he presented many little glasses of those strong liqueurs that flow like pure water into Romanian gullets, "schnaps" which costs less than a penny a glass, and especially "rakiu," a violent plum brandy, which flows freely in the land of the Carpathians.

It should be mentioned that the innkeeper Jonas, as was the custom of the inn, served people only "by the seat," that is to say to people sitting at table, having observed that seated consumers consumed more copiously than standing consumers. That evening, though, things looked promising, since all the stools were claimed by customers. So Jonas went from one table to the other, jug in hand, filling empty tumblers without counting them.

It was 8:30 in the evening. They had been holding forth since dusk, without managing to come to an agreement over what should be done. But these fine fellows all agreed on one point: namely, that if the Castle of the Carpathians was inhabited by unknown people, it was becoming as dangerous for the village of Werst as a powder magazine would be at the entrance to the town.

"It's very serious!" Master Koltz said.

"Very serious!" the schoolmaster replied between two puffs of his inseparable pipe.

"Very serious!" repeated the others in attendance.

"What is only too sure," Jonas began, "is that the castle's bad reputation was already doing great harm to the country...."

"And now it will be something else entirely!" the schoolmaster Hermod cried out.

"Foreigners came here only rarely..." replied Master Koltz, with a sigh.

"And now they won't come at all!" added Jonas, sighing in unison with the *biró*.

"A number of inhabitants are already thinking of leaving!" one of the drinkers observed.

"Me first," a peasant from the neighborhood replied, "and I'll leave as soon as I've sold my vines...."

"For which you'll bankrupt the buyers, my good man!" the innkeeper retorted.

We can see where the conversation of these worthy men was headed. From the personal fears the Castle of the Carpathians caused them, there arose an awareness of their interests, so regrettably damaged. No more travelers, and Jonas would suffer in the income of his inn. No more foreigners, and Master Koltz would suffer in the collection of the toll, the revenue from which was gradually decreasing. No more buyers for the lands of the Vulkan Pass, and the owners wouldn't be able to find anyone to sell them to, even at a ridiculous price. It had been like this for years now, and the situation, already bad, threatened to become even worse.

In fact, if it was this way when the spirits of the castle kept quiet to the point of never letting themselves be seen, what would it be now, if they manifested their presence by material actions?

The shepherd Frik thought that he should say it then, but in a somewhat hesitant voice:

"Maybe we should...?"

"What?" asked Master Koltz.

"Go look at it, master."

Everyone looked at each other, then lowered their eyes, and this question remained unanswered.

It was Jonas who, addressing Master Koltz, spoke again.

"Your shepherd," he said firmly, "has just indicated the only thing there is to be done."

"Go to the castle...."

"Yes, my good friends," the innkeeper replied. "If smoke is coming from the keep's chimney, that's because someone is making a fire there, and if someone is making a fire, it's because a hand lit it...."

"A hand... unless it's a claw!" replied the old peasant, shaking his head.

"Hand or claw," said the innkeeper, "it doesn't matter! We have to know what it means. This is the first time smoke has come from one of the castle's chimneys since Baron Rudolf of Gortz left it...."

"It could be, though, that there was already smoke there before, without anyone noticing it," Master Koltz suggested.

"That is what I'll never admit!" the schoolmaster Hermod shouted with feeling.

"But it's very possible," the *biró* observed, "since we didn't have the telescope to see what was happening in the castle."

This remark was true. The phenomenon could have been going on for a long time, and have escaped even the shepherd Frik, however good his eyes were. Whatever the case, whether said phenomenon was recent or not, it was unarguable that human beings were presently living in the Castle of the Carpathians. And the proximity of this circumstance was unsettling the inhabitants of Vulkan and Werst.

Magister Hermod thought he could use this objection to back up his beliefs:

"Human beings, my friends? Permit me to believe none of that! Why would human beings think of taking refuge in the castle, with what intention would they do so, and how could they have gotten there...?"

"What do you think these intruders are, then?" Master Koltz cried out.

"Supernatural beings," replied Magister Hermod in an imposing voice. "Why shouldn't they be spirits, trolls, goblins, perhaps even some of those dangerous *lamia*, who show themselves in the shapes of beautiful women...."

During this enumeration, everyone's gaze was directed at the door, at the windows, at the chimney of the great room of the King Mathias. And, in truth, everyone wondered if he wasn't going to see one or another of these phantoms appear as they were mentioned in order by the schoolmaster.

"However, my good friends," Jonas risked saying, "if these beings are spirits, that doesn't explain why they would have lit a fire, since they don't have anything to cook...."

"What about their sorceries?" the shepherd replied. "Are you forgetting that you need fire for sorcery?"

"Obviously!" the schoolmaster added in a tone that

didn't tolerate a reply.

This verdict was unquestioningly accepted and, in everyone's opinion, they were without doubt supernatural beings, not human beings, who had chosen the Castle of the Carpathians as a theater for their schemes.

Until now, Nic Deck had taken no part in the conversation. The forester was content to listen attentively to what the others were saying. The old castle, with its mysterious walls, its ancient origin, its feudal bearing, had always inspired as much curiosity as respect in him. He had even, since he was very brave, even though he was just as credulous as any inhabitant of Werst, more than once shown a wish to enter the castle bounds.

As you can imagine, Miriota had stubbornly dissuaded him from such an adventurous project. He could have ideas like that when he was free to act as he liked; but a fiancé no longer belonged to himself, and venturing out on such expeditions would have been the work of a madman, or of someone who just didn't care. And yet, despite her prayers, the beautiful girl always feared lest the forester put his plan into execution. What reassured her a little is that Nic Deck had never formally declared his intention of going to the castle, for no one would have had enough influence over him to keep him back—not even she. She knew him, he was a persistent, resolute young man, who never went back on his word. To say a thing was to do it—once said, once done. So Miriota would have been in agony, if she could have known to what thoughts the young man was abandoning himself at that instant.

However, since Nic Deck kept silent, it follows that the shepherd's proposition was taken up by no one. Who would dare visit the Castle of the Carpathians now that it was haunted, unless he had lost his head? Everyone discovered the best reasons, then, to do nothing about it. The *biró* was no longer of an age to risk his safety on such rough paths.... The schoolmaster had his school to look after, Jonas, his inn to take care of, Frik, his sheep to give pasture to, the other peasants, the business of taking care of their animals and their hay.

No! Not one person would agree to sacrifice himself, repeating to himself:

"Anyone bold enough to go to the castle might never come back!"

At that instant the door to the inn opened suddenly, to the great terror of those present.

It was only Dr. Patak, and it would have been difficult to mistake him for one of those bewitching *lamias* Magister Hermod had spoken of.

His patient having died—which did credit to his medical perspicacity, if not to his talent—Dr. Patak had hurried to the meeting at the King Mathias.

"At last, here he is!" Master Koltz cried out.

Dr. Patak hastened to dispense handshakes to everyone, as he would have dispensed drugs, and in a somewhat ironic tone of voice, he cried out:

"So then, my friends, it's still the castle... the castle of the *Chort*, that takes up your time! Poor cowards! But if this old castle wants to smoke, let it smoke! Doesn't our scholar Hermod smoke, and all day long at that? Truly, the whole countryside is pale with terror! I've heard talk of nothing else but that during my visits! Ghosts have set a fire there? And why not, if they have a head cold! It appears it's freezing in May in the rooms of the keep.... Unless they're busy baking bread for the other world! You have to eat up there, if it's true you come back to life! Maybe they're bakers from heaven, who've come to make a batch...."

A series of jokes ended his little speech, little suited to the people of Werst, which Dr. Patak uttered with an incredible amount of self-satisfaction.

They let him talk.

And then the *biró* asked him:

"Well then, Doctor, you don't attach any importance to what is happening at the castle?"

"None whatsoever, Master Koltz."

"Haven't you said you'd be ready to go there... if you were challenged to?"

"Me?" the former medical attendant replied, not without letting a certain amount of annoyance that he was being reminded of his words show through.

"Come now.... Haven't you said it over and over?" the schoolmaster continued, insisting.

"I did say so... no doubt... and actually... if it's just a question of repeating it...."

"It's a question of doing it," said Hermod.

"Of doing it?

"Yes... and, instead of challenging you to do it, we'll content ourselves with asking you to do it," added Master Koltz.

"You understand... my friends... certainly... such a proposition...."

"Well then, since you hesitate," the innkeeper cried out, "we won't ask you... we'll challenge you!"

"You challenge me?"

"Yes, Doctor!"

"Jonas, you go too far," the *biró* said. "We shouldn't challenge Patak.... We know he is a man of his word.... And what he has said he would do, he will do... even if it's only to do the village and the entire country a favor."

"What's this, are you serious? You want me to go to the Castle of the Carpathians?" the doctor said, whose ruddy face had become very pale.

"There's no way of excusing yourself," Master Koltz categorically replied.

"I beg you... my good friends... I beg you... be reasonable, please!"

"It's quite reasonable," Jonas replied.

"Be fair.... What would be the use of my going there... and what would I find there? A few fine fellows taking refuge in the castle... harming no one...."

"Well then," Magister Hermod replied, "if they're fine fellows, you have nothing to fear from them, and it will be an opportunity to offer them your services."

"If they needed them," Dr. Patak replied, "if they sent for me, I wouldn't hesitate... believe me... to go to the castle. But I never go anywhere without being invited, and I don't make my visits for free...."

"We'll pay you for your trouble," said Master Koltz, "and at whatever hourly rate you like."

"And who will pay me?"

"I will... we will... at whatever rate you name!" most of Jonas's customers answered.

Visibly, despite his constant boasting, the doctor was, to say the least, as much of a coward as his compatriots in Werst. Thus, after he had posed as a man of strong mind, after he had jeered at the legends of the country, he was too embarrassed to refuse the favor he was being asked.

And yet, going to the Castle of the Carpathians, even if he were paid for his visit, was in no way agreeable to him. So he tried to argue that this visit would be fruitless, that the village would be covered in ridicule by delegating him as explorer of the castle.... His argument fizzled out.

"Come now, doctor, it seems to me you have absolutely nothing to risk," Magister Hermod said, "since you don't believe in spirits..."

"No... I don't believe in them."

"But if they're not spirits returning to the castle, they are human beings who have settled there, and you will make their acquaintance."

The reasoning of the schoolmaster didn't lack logic: it was difficult to retort to.

"All right, Hermod," Dr. Patak replied, "but they might keep me at the castle..."

"Then you'll have been well received," Jonas replied.

"No doubt. But what if my absence is prolonged, and someone needs me in the village..."

"We're all in the best of health," Master Koltz replied, "and there hasn't been one single sick person in Werst since your last patient took his ticket for the other world."

"Speak honestly.... Have you decided to go?" asked the innkeeper.

"My word, no!" replied the doctor. "Oh! Not from fear.... You know very well I don't have any faith in all those sorceries.... The truth is that it seems absurd to me, and, I repeat, ridiculous.... Because some smoke has come out of the chimney of the keep... smoke that might not even be smoke.... Definitely... no! I won't go to the Castle of the Carpathians...."

"I will go!"

It was the forester Nic Deck who had just entered the conversation with these few words.

"You... Nic?" cried out Master Koltz.

"Me.... But only on the condition that Patak goes with me."

This was directly addressed to the doctor, who tried at once to extricate himself.

"Do you think so, forester?" he replied. "Me... go with you? Certainly... it would be a pleasant walk to take... the both of us... if there were any purpose to it... and if we chanced to find our way.... Come now, Nic, you know very well there isn't even a road that goes to the castle.... We wouldn't be able to reach it...."

"I said I'd go to the castle," Nic Deck replied, "and since I said so, I'll go."

"But I... I didn't say so!" the doctor cried out struggling, as if someone had seized hold of his collar.

"Yes... you did say so...." Jonas said.

"Yes! Yes!" cried everyone there, in one voice.

The former quarantine attendant, hard-pressed by everyone there, didn't know which way to turn. Now he regretted having so imprudently committed himself by his continual boasting. He would never have imagined they'd take him seriously, or that anyone would be called on to pay for his services.... Now it was no longer possible to slip away without becoming the laughing-stock of Werst, and the entire country of Vulkan would have mercilessly scoffed at him. So he decided to try and make the best of it.

"All right... since you wish it," he said, "I'll go with

Nic Deck, although it will be pointless!"

"Good, very good, Dr. Patak!" all the drinkers at the King Mathias cried out.

"And when will we leave, forester?" asked Dr. Patak, affecting a tone of indifference that scarcely disguised his cowardliness.

"Tomorrow, in the morning," Nic Deck replied.

These last few words were followed by a rather long silence. That showed how real the emotion of Master Koltz and the others was. The glasses had been emptied, the pots too, yet no one got up, no one thought of leaving the main room although it was late, or of returning home. So Jonas thought it was a good opportunity to serve another round of schnapps and *rakiou*...

Suddenly a voice made itself heard distinctly in the midst of the general silence, and these are the words that were slowly uttered:

"*Nicolas Deck, do not go to the castle tomorrow! ...Do not go there... or misfortune will befall you!*"

Who had expressed himself this way? Whence came this voice that no one recognized, and that seemed to come from an invisible mouth? It could only be the voice of a ghost, a supernatural voice, a voice from the other world....

Terror was at its height. No one dared look at each other, or utter a word....

The bravest person—clearly that was Nic Deck—wanted to know what was happening. It was certainly within the room itself that these words had been uttered. And, first of all, the forester had the courage to approach the sideboard and open it....

No one.

He went to inspect the rooms on the ground floor, which communicated with the main room....

No one.

He pushed open the door to the inn, went outside, crossed the terrace as far as the main street of Werst...

No one.

A few instants later, Master Koltz, Magister Hermod, Dr. Patak, Nic Deck, the shepherd Frik, and the others had deserted the inn, leaving only the innkeeper Jonas, who hastened to double-bolt his door.

That night, as if they had been threatened with a fantastic apparition, the inhabitants of Werst barricaded themselves firmly inside their houses....

Terror reigned in the village.

V

The next morning, Nic Deck and Dr. Patak prepared to leave by nine o'clock. The forester's intention was to climb the Vulkan Pass by taking the shortest route towards the suspicious castle.

After the phenomenon of the smoke in the castle keep, after the phenomenon of the voice heard in the main room of the King Mathias, you will not be surprised to learn that the entire population was panic-stricken. Some Gypsies were already talking of leaving the country. Within individual families, that was all that was talked about—and in muted voices. No use even trying to dispute whether or not the devil, the *Chort*, was in that utterance that so threatened the young forester. In Jonas's inn there were about fifteen people—some of them the most credible members of the community— who had heard these strange words. To claim they had been the dupes of some sensory delusion was untenable. There was no doubt in this respect; Nic Deck had been warned, and by name, that misfortune would come to him if he persisted in his plan of exploring the Castle of the Carpathians.

But still the young forester was getting ready to leave Werst, without being forced to do so. In fact, despite whatever advantage Master Koltz might get from clearing up the mystery of the castle, despite whatever interest the village might have in finding out what was happening up there, urgent steps had been taken to try to get Nic Deck to go back on his word. Weeping, desperate, her beautiful eyes drowned in tears, Miriota had begged him not to persist in this adventure. Even before the warning given by the voice, it had already been a serious matter. After the warning, it was insane. And now on the eve of their wedding, Nic Deck wanted to risk his life in such an attempt, and his fiancée, clutching at his knees, couldn't manage to keep him back....

Neither the pleas of his friends nor Miriota's tears were able to influence the forester. But that didn't surprise anyone. They all knew his indomitable character, his tenacity, or should we say his stubbornness. He had said he would go to the Castle of the Carpathians, and nothing could prevent him—not even that threat that had been directly addressed to him. Yes, he would go to the castle, even if he never returned!

When the time came to leave, Nic Deck clasped Miriota to his heart one last time, while the poor girl crossed herself with the thumb, index, and middle finger, following the Romanian custom, which pays homage to the Holy Trinity.

And Dr. Patak...? Well, Dr. Patak, called upon to accompany the forester, had tried to get out of it, but without success. Whatever could be argued, he had argued! Whatever objections were imaginable, he had made them. He had taken refuge behind that formal command not to go to the castle that had been distinctly heard....

"That threat concerns no one but me," Nic Deck had confined himself to saying to him.

"And if some misfortune happens to you, forester," Dr. Patak had replied, "would I get out of it without harm?"

"Harm or no, you promised to come with me to the castle, and you will come, since I am going there!"

Understanding that nothing would prevent him from keeping his promise, the people of Werst had sided with the forester on this point. It was better that Nic Deck not undertake this adventure alone. So the greatly vexed doctor, feeling he couldn't shirk his duty anymore, for to do so would be to compromise his situation in the village and be held in contempt after his customary bragging, gave in, his soul full of fear. But his mind was firmly made up to take advantage of the slightest obstacle in the path that might present itself to force his companion to retrace his steps.

Nic Deck and Dr. Patak set forth, then, and Master Koltz, Magister Hermod, Frik, and Jonas accompanied them to the turn in the main road, where they stopped.

From this spot, Master Koltz aimed his telescope one last time—he was never without it now—in the direction of the castle. No smoke could be seen above the castle keep's chimney, and it would have been easy to perceive it on such a pure horizon, on that fine spring morning. Should they conclude that the natural or supernatural guests of the castle had cleared off, seeing that the forester wasn't heeding their threats? Some thought so, and that was a decisive reason to lead the matter to a satisfactory conclusion.

They shook hands, and Nic Deck, dragging the doctor along, disappeared at the corner of the pass.

The young forester was wearing his official outfit: cap with visor trimmed with braid, belted jacket with sheathed cutlass, baggy trousers, hobnailed boots, cartridge pouch at his waist, long rifle on his shoulder. He had the justified reputation of being a very good shot, and since, even if there were no ghosts, one might encounter some of those prowlers that wander the frontier, or, failing prowlers, some ill-intentioned bear, it was only prudent to be able to defend oneself.

As for the doctor, he had thought he should arm himself with an old flint pistol, which missed three shots out of five. He also carried a hatchet that his companion had equipped him with, since it was likely that it might be necessary to clear a passage through the dense thickets of the Plesa. Wearing the wide hat of country folk, buttoned up under his thick traveling cape, he was shod with elaborately metal-ornamented boots, but all this paraphernalia still wasn't heavy enough to keep him from running away, if the occasion presented itself.

Nic Deck and he had also equipped themselves with some provisions which they carried in their pouch, in order to be able, if necessary, to prolong their exploration.

After passing the turn in the road, Nic Deck and Dr.

Patak walked several hundred feet along the Nyad, climbing its right bank. Following the path that continues through the ravines of the massif would have made them stray too far to the west. It would have been better to be able to continue to walk along the riverbed, which would have reduced the distance by a third, since the Nyad has its source in the innermost reaches of the Plateau of Orgall. But, although it was navigable at first, the bank, deep gouged and blocked by huge rocks, wouldn't let anyone pass, not even travelers on foot. So it was necessary to cut across obliquely to the left, even if it meant heading back later towards the castle, after they had crossed the lower zone of the forests of the Plesa.

That was, in fact, the only side by which the castle was approachable. When it was inhabited by Count Rudolf of Gortz, communication between the village of Werst, the Vulkan Pass, and the valley of the Wallachian Sil was carried out by means of a narrow path that had been opened by following this direction. But, since the path had been abandoned for twenty years to the invasions of vegetation and obstructed by the inextricable jumble of undergrowth, in vain did they search for the trace of a footpath or winding track.

When they abandoned the steep riverbed of the Nyad, which was full of roaring water, Nic Deck paused in order to get his bearings. Already the castle was no longer visible. It would become so only beyond the curtain of forests that were laid out in tiers on the low slopes of the mountain—an arrangement that was common to the whole orographic system of the Carpathians. Orientation would therefore be hard to determine, for lack of landmarks. You could only establish it by the position of the sun, whose rays were just then flushing the distant summits towards the southeast.

"You see, forester," the doctor said, "You see! There isn't even a path... or rather, there isn't one anymore!"

"There will be," Nic Deck replied.

"That's easy to say, Nic...."

"And easy to do, Patak."

"So, you're still determined...?"

The forester contented himself with answering with an affirmative sign and started walking again through the trees.

At that instant, the doctor experienced a strong desire to turn around and go back; but his companion, who had just looked back, gave him such a resolute look that the coward didn't think it wise to linger behind.

Dr. Patak still had one last hope: that Nic Deck would soon get lost in the midst of the labyrinth of these woods, where his service as forester had never brought him. But he hadn't taken into account that wonderful intuition, that professional instinct, that "animal" instinct so to speak, that allows one to be guided by the slightest signs: the projection of branches in one direction or another, the unevenness of the ground, the color of the bark, the variegated shades of moss according to whether they're exposed to winds from the south or the north. Nic Deck was too clever at his profession, he exercised it with too superior a sagacity, ever to get lost, even in places unknown to him. He would have been the worthy rival of a Hawkeye or Chingachgook in Cooper's Leatherstocking country.

Crossing this zone of trees, however, would offer real difficulties. Elms, beeches, some of those maple trees they call "sycamores," superb oaks, occupied the first levels up to the tier of birches, pines, and firs, massed on the upper hilltops on the left side of the pass. These trees were magnificent, with their powerful trunks, their branches warm with new sap, their thick foliage, intertwining with each other to form a canopy of greenery that the sun's rays did not manage to pierce.

The passage would have been relatively easy, though, by winding beneath the low branches. But what obstacles there were on the ground's surface, and what labor would have been necessary to clear the way, to free it from nettles and brambles, to make oneself safe from those thousands of thorns and prickles that the slightest touch tears from them! But Nic Deck was not a man to worry about such things, and, provided he could make his way through the wood, he didn't fuss over a few scratches. Progress, however, could only be very slow in these conditions—an annoying aggravation, since Nic Deck and Dr. Patak would have liked to reach the castle by afternoon. There would still be enough daylight left then to visit it—and that would allow them to be back in Werst before nightfall.

Hatchet in hand, then, the forester worked to clear a way in the midst of these deep thorn bushes, bristling with vegetable bayonets, where his feet encountered an uneven, rough ground, bumpy with roots or stumps, against which he stumbled, when he didn't sink into a wet layer of dead leaves the wind had never swept away. Myriads of pods burst like peas exploding, to the great terror of the doctor, who jumped at this crackling noise, looking right and left, turning round with fear when some climbing vine clung to his jacket, like a claw that wanted to hold him back. No, he wasn't the least bit reassured, the poor man. But now he would not have dared go back alone, and so he tried his best not to let himself be outpaced by his inflexible companion.

Sometimes bright spots appeared capriciously in the forest. A shower of light penetrated it. Pairs of black swans, disturbed in their solitude, flew away from the high boughs, flapping their great wings. Crossing these clearings made walking even more tiring. In some places trees were piled up like an enormous game of pick-up-sticks, blown down by a storm or fallen from old age, as if the lumberjack's axe had given them their death blow. In other places enormous trunks lay, eaten away by rot, that no tool would ever cut into firewood, and no cart would ever drag to the bed of the Wallachian Sil. Facing these obstacles, hard to cross, sometimes impossible to skirt, Nic Deck and his companion were hard pressed. If the young forester—agile, supple, vigorous—managed to get through them, Dr. Patak, with his short legs, his paunchy stomach, out of breath, hoarse, could not avoid some fall, which forced Nic to come to his aid.

"You'll see, Nic, that I'll end up breaking some limb!" he repeated.

"You'll mend it."

"Come, forester, be reasonable.... We shouldn't fling ourselves at the impossible!"

Bah! Nic Deck was already far ahead, and the doctor, getting no results, hurried to join him.

Was the direction they had so far been following the right one that would lead them towards the castle? It would have been difficult to find out. Still, since the ground kept rising, they were nearing the edge of the forest, which they reached at three in the afternoon.

Beyond, up to the Plateau of Orgall, the curtain of green trees stretched, becoming sparser as the slope of the massif gained altitude.

In that place, the Nyad reappeared in the midst of some rocks, either because it had made a bend towards the northwest, or because Nic Deck had borne off towards it. That gave the young forester the certainty that he had chosen the right path, since the stream seemed to spring up from the bowels of the Plateau of Orgall.

Nic Deck could not refuse the doctor an hour's pause by the river's edge. What's more, their stomachs demanded what was due them as imperiously as their legs. Their knapsacks were well provided, and *rakiou* filled the doctor's and Nic Deck's flasks. Moreover, a clear, cool water, filtered by the pebbles in the bottom of the river, flowed a few feet away. What more could they wish for? They had expended a lot; the expense had to be made up for.

Since their departure, the doctor had scarcely had time to chat with Nic Deck, who was always ahead of him. But he made up for that as soon as they were both seated on the bank of the Nyad. If the one was not very talkative, the other was a chatterbox. From that, you will not be surprised that the questions were very wordy, and the answers very brief.

"Let's talk a little, forester, and let's talk seriously," said the doctor.

"I'm listening," replied Nic Deck.

"I think that since we have paused in this place, it's in order to regain our strength."

"Nothing truer."

"Before we return to Werst...."

"No... before we go to the castle."

"Look, Nic, we've been walking for six hours, and we're barely halfway...."

"Which proves we have no time to lose."

"But it will be nighttime when we arrive at the castle, and since I imagine, forester, that you won't be mad enough to risk your safety without being able to see clearly, we'll have to wait till daylight...."

"We'll wait."

"So you don't want to give up this plan, which makes no sense whatever?"

"No."

"What! Here we are, exhausted, needing a good meal in a warm room, and a nice bed in a nice room, and you're thinking of spending the night out in the open?"

"Yes, if some obstacle prevents us from going through the castle wall."

"And if there is no obstacle?"

"We'll go sleep in the rooms in the castle keep."

"The rooms in the castle keep!" Dr. Patak cried out. "Do you think, forester, that I'll agree to stay for a whole night inside that cursed castle...."

"Of course you will, unless you'd rather stay alone outside."

"Alone, forester! That's hardly what we agreed on, and if we have to separate, I'd much rather we do it here, so I can return to the village!"

"What is agreed on, Dr. Patak, is that you follow me wherever I go...."

"During the day, yes! At night, no!"

"Well then, you're free to go, and try not to get lost

under the stands of trees."

Getting lost is precisely what the doctor was worried about. Left on his own, unfamiliar with these interminable winding paths through the forests of the Plesa, he felt incapable of finding the way to Werst again. What's more, being alone when night had fallen—possibly a very dark night—descending the slopes of the pass at the risk of falling to the bottom of a ravine, wasn't to his liking. As long as it didn't mean climbing the battlement when the sun had set, if the forester persisted, it was better to follow him to the foot of the outer wall. But the doctor wanted to make one last attempt to stop his companion.

"You know very well, my dear Nic," he went on, "that I will never agree to be separated from you.... Since you persist in going to the castle, I won't let you go there alone."

"Well spoken, Dr. Patak, and I think you should continue in that vein."

"No... one word more, Nic. If it's night when we arrive, promise me you won't try to penetrate into the castle...."

"What I do promise you, Doctor, is to do the impossible to penetrate it, not to move an inch back, as long as I haven't discovered what's going on there."

"What's going on there!" Dr. Patak mocked, shrugging his shoulders. "What do you think is going on there, forester?"

"I have no idea, and since I've made up my mind to find out, I'll find out...."

"But we still have to be able to get there, to that devil's castle!" the doctor replied, who had run out of arguments. "And, judging from the difficulties we've encountered till now, and from the time we've spent crossing the forests of the Plesa, the day will be over before we're in sight of...."

"I'm not thinking about that," Nic Deck replied. "On top of the massif, the firs are less overgrown than these clusters of elms, maples, and beeches."

"But the ground will be hard to climb!"

"What does that matter, if it isn't impassable."

"But I've heard it said that there are bears around the Plateau of Orgall!"

"I have my rifle, and you have your pistol to defend yourself, Doctor."

"But if night falls, we might get lost in the darkness!"

"No, since now we have a guide—one, I hope, that won't abandon us anymore."

"A guide?" the doctor cried.

And he quickly got up to glance worriedly around him.

"Yes," Nic Deck replied, "and this guide is the Nyad river. We just have to climb its right bank to reach the very summit of the plateau, where it has its source. So I think that we'll be at the door of the castle before two hours are up, if we set out again without delay."

"In two hours, unless it's in six!"

"Come on, then, are you ready?"

"Already, Nic, already? But our rest has barely lasted a few minutes!"

"A few minutes that are a good half-hour. For the last time, are you ready?"

"Ready... when my legs are heavy as blocks of lead... You know very well I don't have your strong forester's legs, Nic Deck! My feet are swollen, and it's cruel to force me to follow you...."

"You're beginning to annoy me, Patak! You have my permission to go and leave me! Farewell."

And Nic Deck got up.

"For the love of God, forester," Dr. Patak cried out, "listen to me a little more!"

"Listen to your ramblings?"

"Look, since it's already late, why not stay in this place, why not set up camp under the shelter of these trees? We could leave tomorrow at dawn, and we'd have all morning to reach the plateau...."

"Doctor," replied Nic Deck, "let me repeat that I intend to spend the night in the castle."

"No!" cried the doctor, "No.... You won't do it, Nic! I'll prevent you...."

"You?"

"I'll cling to you.... I'll drag you away! I'll beat you, if I have to...."

He no longer knew what he was saying, the unfortunate Patak.

As for Nic Deck, he didn't even answer him, and, after putting his rifle back in his bandoleer, he took a few steps, heading towards the bank of the Nyad.

"Wait... wait!" the doctor cried out piteously. "What a devil of a man! One more instant! My legs are stiff... my joints aren't functioning...."

They weren't long in not functioning, however, since the ex-attendant had to scamper along on his little legs to join the forester, who didn't even turn around.

It was four o'clock. The sun's rays, touching the ridge of the Plesa, which would soon block them, lit up the tall branches of the forest with a slanting beam of light. Nic Deck was perfectly right to hurry, since these lower parts of the forests soon got dark at the end of day.

These woods, where alpine essences were gathered, had a curious, weird look. Instead of twisted, lopsided, grimacing trees, straight trunks rose up, well spaced-out, bare up to fifty or sixty feet above their roots: trunks without knots, stretching out their persistent greenery like a ceiling. Not much scrub or tangled grass at their base. Long roots, crawling just above the ground, like snakes numb from the cold. A forest floor covered with a yellowish, dense and compact moss, interwoven with dry twigs and scattered with fruits that crackled underfoot. A steep embankment furrowed with crystalline rocks, whose sharp edges bit into the thickest leather. So the way through this fir forest was hard for a quarter of a mile. To climb these blocks, you needed a strong back, vigorous knees, sureness of limbs—all of which had deserted Dr. Patak. Nic Deck would have taken no more than an hour if he'd been alone, but it cost him three with the hindrance of his companion, having to stop to wait for him, helping to hoist him up some rock too tall for his little legs. The doctor just had one fear left now, a terrifying fear: that of finding himself alone in the midst of these gloomy solitudes.

However, though these slopes were becoming more difficult to climb, the trees were beginning to become fewer on the high summit of the Plesa. They were now only isolated stands, of average height. Between these stands, one could see the line of mountains that appeared in the background, whose lineaments were still visible in the evening mist.

The Nyad river, alongside which the forester had been walking all this while, dwindled down to being nothing more than a stream; the source from which it rose was not far ahead. A few hundred feet above the last bends in the terrain the Plateau of Orgall rose and leveled off, crowned by the castle buildings.

Nic Deck finally reached this plateau, after a final backbreaking effort that reduced the doctor to an inert mass. The poor man wouldn't have had the strength to drag himself twenty feet more, and he fell down like a slaughtered steer beneath the butcher's axe.

Nic Deck scarcely felt tired from this difficult climb. Upright, immobile, he hungrily eyed the Castle of the Carpathians, which he had never come near before.

In front of him, a crenellated wall stretched wide, defended by a deep ditch, whose only drawbridge was raised against a barbican, surrounded by a ring of stones.

Around the wall, on the surface of the Plateau of Orgall, everything was deserted and silent.

A remnant of daylight allowed his gaze to embrace the whole of the castle, which became confusedly blurred in the evening's shadows. No one could be seen above the parapet of the fortified wall, no one on the upper platform of the castle keep, or on the circular terrace of the upper storey. Not one plume of smoke coiled round the extravagant weathervane, eaten away by age-old rust.

"Well then, forester," asked Dr. Patak, "will you agree it's impossible to cross this ditch, to lower the drawbridge, and to open that barbican?"

Nic Dick did not reply. He realized it would be necessary to camp overnight in front of the castle walls. In the midst of this darkness, how would he be able to descend to the bottom of the ditch and climb up the other side to penetrate the wall? Obviously, the wisest thing was to wait for the coming dawn, in order to act in full daylight.

That was what was resolved, to the great annoyance of the forester, but to the extreme satisfaction of the doctor.

VI

The slim crescent of the moon, loosed like a silver sickle, had disappeared almost immediately after sunset. Clouds, coming in from the west, one by one extinguished the last glimmer of dusk. Darkness slowly invaded space, climbing up from the lower zones. The mountain cirque was filled with shadows, and the shapes of the castle soon vanished beneath the veil of night.

Although the night threatened to be dark, there was no sign it would be disturbed by any kind of atmospheric disturbances, thunderstorms, rain, or gales. That was fortunate for Nic Deck and his companion, who were about to camp out in the open.

There were no stands of trees on this arid Plateau of Orgall. Here and there were a few close-cropped bushes, lying close to the ground, and they offered no shelter from the nighttime cold. There were rocks aplenty, some half buried in the ground, others scarcely balanced, which a slight shove would have been enough to topple, making them roll down to the forest.

Actually, the only plant that grew in profusion on this rocky soil was a thick thistle called a "Russian thorn," the seeds of which, says Elisée Reclus, were carried there by Muscovite horsemen in the hides of their steeds—"a present of joyous conquest that the Russians gave the Transylvanians."

Now they had to find some place to wait for day and protect themselves from the drop in temperature, which is quite considerable at that altitude.

"We have plenty of choices... to be uncomfortable!" murmured Dr. Patak.

"Are you complaining, again?" Nic Deck said.

"I certainly am! What a pleasant place to catch a nice cold or some nice rheumatism I won't be able to cure!"

Here was a confession stripped of artifice from the mouth of the former quarantine attendant. Oh, how he missed his comfortable little house in Werst, with its cozy bedroom and its bed piled with pillows and comforters!

Among the boulders scattered about the Plateau of Orgall, they had to pick one whose position offered the best screen against the wind from the southwest, which was just beginning to sting. This is what Nic Deck did, and soon the doctor came to join him behind a large rock, flat like a tablet on top.

This rock was one of those stone slabs, buried beneath scabious and saxifrage, which are commonly found at bends in the road in the Wallachian countryside. While the traveler can sit down on them, he can also quench his thirst with the water contained in a vase placed atop it, which is renewed every day by the country folk. When the castle was inhabited by Baron Rudolf of Gortz, this bench carried a container that the family servants were careful never to leave empty. But now it was soiled with detritus and covered with green mold, and the slightest shock would have reduced it to dust.

At the end of the bench a column of granite rose up, the remnant of an ancient cross, whose arms were represented on the vertical branch only by a half-effaced groove. Dr. Patak, as a freethinker, could not admit that this cross would protect him from supernatural apparitions. Yet, by an anomaly common to a good number of unbelievers, he was not far from believing in the devil. And in his way of thinking, the *Chort* must not have been far away; it was he who haunted the castle, and neither the closed barbican, nor the raised drawbridge, nor the sheer fortified wall, nor the deep ditch, would prevent the devil from coming forth, if the whim seized him to come and twist both their necks.

And when the doctor reflected that he had an entire night to spend in these conditions, he trembled with terror. No! It was too much to ask of a human being, and even the most energetic temperaments could not stand up to it.

Then an idea came belatedly to him—an idea that had not occurred to him before, when he left Werst. It was Tuesday night, and, on that day, the people of the district took care not to go out after sunset. Tuesday, as everyone knows, is the day of evil spells. Judging from tradition, you would be exposing yourself to encountering some malevolent spirit if you ventured forth into the

countryside. So on Tuesdays no one walks on the roads or
the paths after sunset. And now Dr. Patak found himself
not only away from his house, but next to a haunted castle, and two or three miles away from the village! And
that's where he'd be forced to wait for the return of
dawn... if it ever returned! Really, it was like deliberate-
ly tempting the devil!

As he abandoned himself to these thoughts, the doctor saw the forester calmly pull out a piece of cold meat
from his bag, after taking a long drink from his flask. The
best thing he could do, he thought, was to imitate him,
and that's what he did. A thigh of goose, a big chunk of
bread, all washed down with *rakiou*—he needed nothing
less to restore his strength. But, though he managed to
calm his hunger, he did not manage to calm his fear.

"Now let's go to sleep," said Nic Deck, as soon as he
had stored his bag at the foot of the rock.

"Sleep, forester!"

"Good night, Doctor."

"Good night, that's easy to say, but I'm afraid this
night will have a bad ending...."

Nic Deck, scarcely in the mood to chat, did not
answer. Used to sleeping in the middle of the woods,
thanks to his profession, he rested as comfortably as he
could against the stone bench, and soon fell into a profound slumber. The doctor could only grumble with
clenched teeth when he heard his companion's regular
breathing.

As for him, it was impossible for him to annihilate his
senses of hearing and sight even for a few minutes.
Despite his fatigue, he kept looking, and kept listening.
His brain was prey to those extravagant visions that are

born from the confusions of insomnia. What was he trying to see in the dense shadows? Everything and nothing, the vague shapes of the objects surrounding him, the
ragged clouds in the sky, the scarcely perceptible mass of
the castle. Then it was the rocks themselves on the
Plateau of Orgall which seemed to him to move in a kind
of infernal dance. What if they were shaken from their
foundation, hurtled down the length of the talus, rolled
onto these two foolhardy men, and crushed them at the
gate of this castle, the entry to which was forbidden
them!

He got up, the poor doctor, and listened to those
noises that abound on the surface of high plateaus, those
unsettling murmurs, that at once resemble whispering,
moaning, and sighing. He also heard the nyctalops brush-
ing against the rocks with frenetic wingbeats, the strigia
flying on their nocturnal promenade, two or three pairs of
those funereal owls, whose hooting resounded like a
moan. Then his muscles contracted all at once, and his
body shook, bathed in an icy transudation, or cold sweat.

Thus the long hours passed till midnight. If Dr. Patak
had been able to talk, to exchange a comment now and
then, to give free rein to his recriminations, he would
have felt less frightened. But Nic Deck was sleeping,
and he was sleeping a deep sleep. Midnight—that was
the most terrifying time of all, the hour of apparitions,
the hour of evil spells.

Now what was happening?

The doctor had just gotten up, wondering if he was
awake, or if he was under the influence of a nightmare.

In fact, up above, he thought he saw—no! he actually saw—strange forms, lit up in a spectral light, passing

from one horizon to the other, rising, lowering, descending with the clouds. They looked like different kinds of monsters, dragons with serpent tails, hippogriffs with wide wings, giant krakens, enormous vampires, which were swooping down as if to seize him with their claws or gobble him up in their jaws.

Then, everything seemed to be in movement on the Plateau of Orgall—the rocks, the trees that stood at its edge. And very distinctly, clanging noises, at short intervals, reached his ears.

"The bell..." he murmured, "the castle bell!"

Yes! It was indeed the bell of the old chapel, and not that of the church in Vulkan, whose sounds the wind would have carried in an opposite direction.

And now its clanging noises were speeding up.... The hand that was setting it in motion was not sounding a death knell! No! It was an alarm bell whose heaving rings awakened echoes on the Transylvanian border.

Hearing these lugubrious vibrations, Dr. Patak was seized with spasms of fear, insurmountable anxiety, irresistible terror, that made cold shivers run all over his body.

But the forester too had been awakened from his sleep by the terrifying volleys of the bell. He got up, while Dr. Patak seemed to have retreated into himself.

Nic Deck listened carefully, and his eyes tried to pierce the thick shadows that covered the castle.

"That bell! That bell!" Dr. Patak kept repeating. "It's the *Chort* that's ringing it!"

Decidedly, he believed now more than ever in the devil, the poor absolutely terrified doctor!

The forester, motionless, did not reply.

All of a sudden, howls, like those emitted by seaside sirens at the entrance to harbors, exploded in tumultuous waves. The space all around was shaken by their deafening sounds.

Then a bright light shot forth from the central keep, an intensely bright light, which gave forth brilliant scintillations, blinding coruscations. What fireplace could produce such powerful light, whose irradiations wavered over the surface of the Plateau of Orgall in long sheets? From what furnace could that photogenic source escape, which seemed to set fire to the rocks as it bathed them in weird lividity?

"Nic... Nic!" the doctor shouted, "Look at me! Don't I look just like a corpse now?"

In fact, the forester and he had both taken on a cadaverous look, with pale faces, dead eyes, empty sockets, grayish-green cheeks, and their hair looked like the moss that grows, according to legend, on the skulls of hanged men....

Nic Deck was stunned by what he saw, as well as by what he heard. Dr. Patak had reached the last stage of terror; his muscles were contracted, his hairs standing on end, his pupils dilated, his body seized by a tetanic rigidity. As the poet of *Contemplations* says, his "very breath was fear"!

This horrible phenomenon lasted for a minute—a minute at most. Then the strange light gradually weakened, the roar subsided, and the Plateau of Orgall returned to silence and darkness.

Neither of the two men tried to sleep any more; the doctor, overwhelmed by astonishment, and the forester, standing against the stone bench, waited the return of dawn.

What was Nic Deck thinking about, faced with things that were, in his eyes, so obviously supernatural? Wasn't there enough there to shake his resolution? Would he stubbornly persist in pursuing this rash adventure? True, he had said he would penetrate the castle, and explore the keep.... But wasn't it enough to have come up to its impassable wall, to have endured the wrath of the spirits and provoked the anger of the elements? Would he be reproached for not keeping his promise if he returned to the village, without having pushed madness to the point of venturing into this diabolical castle?

All of a sudden, the doctor rushed over to him, seized his hand, and tried to drag him away, repeating in a low voice:

"Come on! Come on!"

"No!" replied Nic Deck.

And he in turn held back Dr. Patak, who collapsed after this final effort.

That night finally came to an end, and such was their mental state that neither the forester nor the doctor was aware of the time that passed till sunrise. They could remember nothing of the hours that preceded the first glimmers of morning.

At that instant, a rosy trace was sketched on the peak of Paring, on the eastern horizon, on the far side of the valley of the two Sils. Pale whiteness spread at the zenith over a background of sky striped like a zebra. Nic Deck turned towards the castle. He saw its forms grow gradually more distinct, the keep stand out from the high mist that was rolling down the Vulkan Pass, then the chapel, galleries, and crenellated walls emerge from the night-time fog; then, on the corner bastion, the beech tree was outlined, its leaves rustling in the easterly breeze.

Nothing had changed in the castle's ordinary appearance. The bell was as motionless as the old feudal weathervane. No smoke curled up from the chimneys of the keep, whose barred windows were obstinately closed.

Some birds flitted about over the platform, uttering clear little calls.

Nic Deck turned his gaze to the castle's main entrance. The drawbridge, raised against the opening, sealed the barbican between the two stone pilasters escutcheoned with the arms of the barons of Gortz.

Was the forester still determined to push this adventurous expedition to the end? Yes, and his resolution had not been dented in the least by the events of the night. No sooner said than done—that was his motto, as we know. Neither the mysterious voice that had threatened him by name in the taproom of the King Mathias nor the inexplicable phenomena of sounds and light he had just witnessed could prevent him from going through the castle wall. An hour would be enough for him to walk through the galleries, visit the keep, and then, his promise carried out, he would take the path to Werst, which he could reach before noon.

As for Dr. Patak, he was now nothing more than an inert machine, having no strength either to resist or even to wish. He would go wherever he was pushed. If he fell, it would have been impossible for him to get back up. The terrors of that night had reduced him to the most complete state of stupor, and he said nothing when the forester, pointing to the castle, said to him, "Let's go!"

Yet daylight had come back, and the doctor could easily have gone back to Werst, without any fear of getting lost in the forests of the Plesa. But we shouldn't attribute his decision to stay with Nic Deck to any sense of duty. If he did not abandon his companion and take the road to the village, it was because he was no longer aware of the situation; he was nothing but a soulless body. Thus, when the forester pulled him towards the embankment of the counterscarp, he let himself be pulled.

Now was there any way of penetrating the castle through some means other than the barbican? That's what Nic Deck wanted to find out.

The outer wall showed no breach, no crumbling, no rift, that could give access to the interior of the enceinte. It was in fact surprising that these old walls were in such a good state of preservation—which must have been owing to their thickness. To climb up to the crenellations that topped them seemed impracticable, since they rose to about forty feet above the moat. So it seemed that Nic Deck, when he had finally reached the Castle of the Carpathians, was about to come up against insurmountable obstacles.

Fortunately—or unfortunately for him—there was over the barbican a kind of loophole, or rather an embrasure, where the muzzle of a culverin used to rest. Now, by using one of the drawbridge chains that hung to the ground, it would not be very difficult for an agile, strong man to hoist himself up to this embrasure. His girth was slim enough to let him through, and, unless it was barred by a grille on the inside, Nic Deck would undoubtedly manage to get into the courtyard of the castle.

The forester understood at first glance that there was

no other way to proceed, and that is why, followed by the benumbed doctor, he took a steep slanting path down the opposite bank of the counterscarp.

Both of them had soon reached the bottom of the ditch, littered with stones and tangled with wild plants. It was hard to tell where they should set foot, and whether myriads of venomous creatures weren't swarming beneath the grass of this damp excavation.

In the center of the ditch, parallel to the wall, was the bed of the ancient moat, almost completely dried out, which could be crossed in one long stride.

Nic Deck, having lost none of his physical or moral energy, acted calmly, while the doctor followed him mechanically, like an animal being pulled by a rope.

After crossing the moat, the forester walked alongside the base of the outer wall for about twenty feet, and stopped beneath the barbican, at the place where the end of the chain was hanging. By using both feet and hands, he could easily reach the stone cordon that jutted out beneath the embrasure.

Of course, Nic Deck wasn't planning on forcing Dr. Patak to attempt this climb with him. So heavy a man would not have been capable of it. So he confined himself to shaking the doctor vigorously to make him understand, and urged him to stay at the bottom of the ditch without moving.

Then Nic Deck began to climb the chain, and it was child's play for his mountaineer's muscles.

But when the doctor saw he was alone, suddenly the awareness of his situation returned to him to some degree. He understood, he looked about, he saw his companion already hanging a dozen feet above the ground, and then he began to shout, his voice strangled in the throes of fear:

"Stop—Nic—stop!"

The forester didn't listen to him.

"Come back—come back—or I'll leave" moaned the doctor, who managed to get up on his feet.

"Go away!" Nic Deck replied.

And he continued to climb slowly along the draw-bridge chain.

Dr. Patak, in a paroxysm of terror, wanted then to regain the steep path of the counterscarp, in order to climb back up to the top of the Plateau of Orgall and make a bolt for the path to Werst....

Oh wonder of wonders, which now blotted out all those that had disturbed the previous night! Now he couldn't move a single inch.... His feet were held rigid as if they were clamped in the jaws of a vise.... Could he put one in front of the other? No! They were stuck by the heels and soles of his boots.... Had the doctor let himself get caught in the teeth of some sort of trap, then? He was too panicked to find out.... It seemed actually as if he was held back by the nails of his shoes.

Whatever the case was, the poor man was frozen in place.... He was rooted to the spot.... Lacking even the strength to cry out, he desperately stretched out his hands.... He looked as if he wanted to tear himself away from the clutches of some kind of *tarasque*, or river drag-on, whose jaws were emerging from the bowels of the earth....

Meanwhile, Nic Deck had reached the top of the bar-bican, and had just placed his hand on one of the handles where one of the hinges of the drawbridge was housed.

A shout of pain escaped him; then, hurling himself back as if he had been struck by lightning, he slid back down the chain, which one last instinct had made him grasp again, and rolled down to the bottom of the ditch.

"The voice did tell me harm would come my way!" he murmured as he lost consciousness.

VII

How can the anxiety that preyed on the village of Werst ever since the departure of the young forester and Dr. Patak be described? It had continued to grow as the seemingly interminable hours passed.

Master Koltz, the innkeeper Jonas, Magister Hermod, and a few others never left the terrace. Each of them stubbornly kept watching the distant mass of the castle, looking to see if any curl of smoke reappeared over the keep. No smoke could be seen—which was noted with the help of the telescope, as was invariably kept aimed in that direction. In truth, the two florins that had been spent to acquire this device was money put to good use. Never did the *biró* have the least bit of regret for such a useful expense—careful though he was, and watchful of his purse.

At 12:30, when the shepherd Frik returned from the

pasture, he was eagerly questioned. Was there anything new, extraordinary, supernatural...?

Frik replied that he had just crossed the valley of the Wallachian Sil, without having seen anything suspicious.

After lunch, around two o'clock, everyone returned to his observation post. No one would have thought of staying at home, and above all no one thought of setting foot in the King Mathias again, where threatening voices had been heard. That walls have ears, that's not so bad, since it's a commonly used phrase in everyday language... but a mouth!

Thus the worthy innkeeper had reason to fear that his tavern might be placed in quarantine, and that worried him to no end. Would he be forced, then, to close up shop, to drink his own supply, for lack of customers? And yet, in order to reassure the population of Werst, he had undertaken a long investigation of the King Mathias, searched all the bedrooms, even under the beds, looked into the chests and dresser, carefully explored all the nooks and crannies of the main room, the cellar, and the attic, where some hoaxer might have organized this mystification. Nothing! Nor was there anything on the side of the façade that looked out over the Nyad. The windows were too high up for anyone to climb up to the opening, on the other side of a sheer wall the base of which plunged into the impetuous torrent of the river. No matter! Fear doesn't reason, and a long time would surely have to pass before Jonas's usual customers had restored their confidence in his inn, his schnapps, and his *rakiou*.

A long time? Wrong, and, as we'll see, this unfortunate prediction would not at all be fulfilled.

In fact, a few days later, owing to a quite unforeseen circumstance, the foremost inhabitants of the village would resume their daily meetings, intermingled with some pleasant glassfuls, at the tables of the King Mathias.

But we must return to the young forester and his companion, Dr. Patak.

As we remember, when he left Werst, Nic Deck had promised the despairing Miriota that he wouldn't extend his visit to the Castle of the Carpathians. If no misfortune befell him, if the threats thundered against him did not come true, he counted on returning to the village by early evening. So the people awaited him, and with such impatience! Neither the young lady, nor her father, nor the schoolmaster had been able to foresee that difficulties on the trail hadn't allowed the forester to reach the summit of the Plateau of Orgall before nightfall.

Hence the anxiety, already so keen throughout the day, surpassed all bounds, when the Vulkan bell (which could be heard quite distinctly in the village of Werst) sounded eight o'clock. What could have happened, that Nic Deck and the doctor had not reappeared after a day's absence? No one would think to return home before they had come back. Every minute, people kept thinking they saw them appearing at the turn of the path on the pass.

Master Koltz and his daughter had gone to the end of the street, to the place where the shepherd had been set to watch. Countless times, they thought they saw shadows taking shape in the distance, through the clearings in the trees.... Pure illusion! The pass was deserted, as usual, for it was rare for people from the border to want to venture there during the night. And remember, it was

Tuesday night—the Tuesday of harmful spirits—and on that day Transylvanians do not willingly travel the countryside at sunset. Nic Deck had to have been crazy to have chosen such a day to visit the castle. The truth is that the young forester hadn't thought about it at all; nor had anyone in the village.

But that is just what Miriota was thinking about now. And what terrifying images appeared to her! In her imagination, she had followed her betrothed hour by hour, through those dense forests of the Plesa, while he was climbing towards the Plateau of Orgall.... Now that night had come, it seemed to her that she saw him inside the enceinte, trying to escape from the spirits that haunted the Castle of the Carpathians.... He had become the plaything of their evil spells.... He was a victim doomed to their revenge.... He was imprisoned at the bottom of some underground oubliette... dead perhaps....

Poor girl, what would she not have given to follow in the footsteps of Nic Deck! Still, since she was unable to, at least she would have liked to wait for him all night right in that place. But her father forced her to go home, and, leaving the shepherd at his post, both father and daughter returned to their house.

As soon as she was alone in her little bedroom, Miriota abandoned herself unreservedly to her tears. She loved him, with all her soul, her brave Nic, and loved him all the more because of her gratitude—since the young forester hadn't sought her hand in the conditions by which marriages in these Transylvanian countries were usually decided, and in such a strange fashion.

Every year, at the Feast of St. Peter, the "fair of betrothal" opens. On that day, there is a meeting of all the young women in the district. They have come with their most beautiful carts harnessed to their best horses; they have brought their dowry, that is to say clothes that were spun, sewn, embroidered with their own hands, locked up in brilliantly colored chests; families, friends, and neighbors accompanied them. And then the young men arrive, dressed in superb suits, belted with silk sashes. They stalk through the fair strutting about; they choose the girl they like; they give her a ring and a handkerchief as a sign of their engagement, and the weddings take place at the end of the festival.

It was not at one of those markets that Nicolas Deck had met Miriota. Their liaison had not occurred by chance. Both of them had known each other since childhood; they had loved each other since they were old enough to love. The young forester had not gone to a fair to seek the one who would be his wife, and Miriota was grateful to him for that. Ah! Why was Nic Deck so resolute, so stubborn, so insistent on keeping a rash promise! He loved her, though, he loved her, and still she hadn't had enough influence to prevent him from setting out for the cursed castle!

What a night the sad Miriota spent in the midst of her anguish and tears! She didn't want to go to bed at all. Leaning out her window, her gaze fixed on the rising street, it seemed to her she could hear a voice murmuring:

"Nicolas Deck did not pay heed to the threats! Miriota has no more betrothed!"

A mistake of her confused senses. No voice traveled through the silence of the night. The inexplicable phenomenon of the room at the King Mathias was not being reproduced in Master Koltz's house.

The next day, at dawn, the entire population of Werst was outside. From the terrace to the turn in the pass, some climbed, others descended the main street—some to ask for news, others to give it. They said the shepherd Frik had just gone ahead, a good mile away from the village, not through the forests of the Plesa, but following their edge, and that he hadn't done so without good reason.

They had to wait, and, so that they could communicate more quickly with him, Master Koltz, Miriota, and Jonas went to the edge of the village.

Half an hour later, Frik was spotted a few hundred feet away, at the top of the road.

Since he didn't seem to be hurrying, this was taken as a bad sign.

"Well, Frik, what have you found out? What did you learn?" Master Koltz asked him, as soon as the shepherd had rejoined them.

"I didn't see anything.... I didn't find out anything!" Frik answered.

"Nothing!" the young woman murmured, whose eyes filled with tears.

"At the break of day," the shepherd resumed, "I had glimpsed two men a mile from here. First I thought it was Nic Deck, accompanied by the doctor... but it wasn't him!"

"Do you know who they were?" Jonas asked.

"Two foreign travelers who had just crossed the Wallachian border."

"Did you speak to them?"

"Yes."

"Did they go down into the village?"

"No, they're headed in the direction of Mt. Retyezat, they want to reach the summit."

"Are they two tourists?"

"They seem like it, Master Koltz."

"And, last night, when they were crossing the Vulkan Pass, they didn't see anything at the castle?"

"No... since they were still on the other side of the border," Frik replied.

"So you have no news of Nic Deck?"

"None."

"Oh my God!" sighed the poor Miriota.

"Still, you can question those travelers in a few days," Frik added, "since they plan on stopping over in Werst, before leaving again for Kolosvar."

Provided no one tells them anything bad about my inn! thought Jonas, inconsolable. They might decide not to put up there!

And for thirty-six hours, the excellent innkeeper was obsessed by this fear that no traveler would dare ever after eat or sleep at the King Mathias.

In short, these questions and these answers, exchanged between the shepherd and his master, had done nothing to shed light on the situation. And since neither the young forester nor Dr. Patak had reappeared at eight in the morning, was there any reason to hope they would ever return...? That is why one can't approach the Castle of the Carpathians with impunity!

Broken by the emotions of that night of insomnia, Miriota had lost the strength to support herself. Faint, she could scarcely manage to walk. Her father had to bring her back home. There, her tears redoubled. She called for Nic in a heartrending voice.... She wanted to go and find him.... Everyone pitied her, and there was reason to fear she might fall ill.

It was necessary, however, and urgent, to make a decision. A search party had to go to the aid of the forester and doctor without losing an instant. That there were dangers to be run by exposing themselves to the retaliation of the unknown beings, human or otherwise, that occupied the castle, it mattered little. The main thing was to find out what had become of Nic Deck and the doctor. This duty was just as clear to their friends as it was to the other inhabitants of the village. Only the bravest would not refuse to plunge into the dense forests of the Plesa to climb up to the Castle of the Carpathians.

Once that was decided, after many discussions and suggestions, the bravest numbered three: Master Koltz, the shepherd Frik, and the innkeeper Jonas—not one more. As to the schoolmaster Hermod, he had suddenly come down with a painful case of gout in his leg, and he had had to lie down across two chairs in his school class-room.

Around nine o'clock, Master Koltz and his companions, prudently well-armed, set off up the path to the Vulkan Pass. Then, in the very place where Nic Deck had left it, they abandoned it, to plunge beneath the dense massif.

They told themselves, not without reason, that if the young forester and the doctor were on their way back to the village, they would be taking the path they had had to follow through the Plesa. They thought it would be easy to spot their tracks, and that was found to be true, as soon as all three had crossed the border of the trees.

We will let them continue on their way, and turn to consider what sort of change of opinion occurred in Werst, as soon as they had lost them from sight. Though it had seemed absolutely necessary for people of good-will to find their way to Nic Deck and Patak, now that they had gone it was deemed an unspeakable foolishness. What a fine result that will be, when the first catastrophe is topped by another! No one doubted anymore that the forester and the doctor had been victims of their attempt, so what was the use of Master Koltz, Frik, and Jonas exposing themselves to becoming the victims of their duty? What would have been accomplished, if the young lady had to mourn her father as she mourned her fiancé, and when the friends of the shepherd and of the innkeeper had to blame themselves for their loss!

Despair became general in Werst, and there was no sign of it abating anytime soon. Even if no harm came to them, they couldn't expect the return of Master Koltz or his two companions before night had enveloped the surrounding summits.

How surprising it was, then, when they were glimpsed around two o'clock in the afternoon, on the road, in the distance! And with what haste did Miriota, who was told immediately, run to meet them.

There weren't three of them, but four, and the fourth turned out to be the doctor.

"Nic... my poor Nic!" the young woman cried out. "Isn't Nic there?"

Yes... Nic Deck was there, laid out on a stretcher of branches that Jonas and the shepherd carried with difficulty.

Miriota rushed towards her fiancé, leaned over him,

clasped him in her arms.

"He is dead!" she cried, "he is dead!"

"No... he is not dead," Dr. Patak replied, "but he should be... and me too!"

The truth is that the young forester had lost consciousness. His limbs were stiff, his face bloodless, his breathing scarcely lifted his chest. As for the doctor, if his face wasn't drained of color like his companion's, that was because the walk had given him back his usual brick-red complexion.

Miriota's voice, so tender, so heartrending, was not able to rouse Nic Deck from the torpor into which he was plunged. When he had been brought back to the village and placed in Master Koltz's bedroom, he hadn't yet uttered one single word. A few moments later, though, his eyes opened, and, as soon as he saw the girl leaning over his bed, a smile played on his lips; but when he tried to get up, he could not manage it. Part of his body was paralyzed, as if he had been struck with hemiplegia. Still, wanting to reassure Miriota, he said to her, in a weak voice:

"It's nothing.... Nothing!"

"Nic—my poor Nic!" the girl said over and over.

"It's just a little exhaustion, my dear Miriota, and a little emotion.... It will be over soon... with your care...."

But the invalid needed calm and rest. So Master Koltz left the room, leaving Miriota beside the young forester, who could not have wished for a more diligent nurse, and soon dozed off.

During this time, the innkeeper Jonas proclaimed to a large audience and in a loud voice, so that he could be heard by all, what had happened since their departure.

After they had discovered the path that Nic Deck and the doctor had cleared through the woods, Master Koltz, the shepherd, and Jonas had headed in the direction of the Castle of the Carpathians. For two hours they climbed the slopes of the Plesa, and the edge of the forest was no more than half a mile in front of them, when the two men appeared. It was the doctor, who was exhausted and had just fallen down at the foot of a tree, and the forester, who couldn't get his legs to move.

In no time at all they had run up to the doctor and questioned him—but without getting even a single word in reply, since he was too dazed to answer. They made a stretcher out of branches, lay Nic Deck down onto it, and got Patak back on his feet. Then Master Koltz and the shepherd, spelled sometimes by Jonas, had taken the path back to Werst.

As to why Nic Deck was in such a state, and whether he had explored the castle ruins, the innkeeper didn't know any more than Master Koltz or the shepherd Frik did, since the doctor hadn't recovered his spirits enough to satisfy their curiosity.

But if Patak hadn't spoken till then, he had to speak now. Good gracious! He was safe in his village, surrounded by his friends, in the midst of his patients! He had nothing more to fear from the beings over there! Even if they had made him swear to keep silent, to tell nothing of what he had seen at the Castle of the Carpathians, public interest commanded him to break his oath.

"Come now, come to your senses, Doctor," Master Koltz said to him, "and tell us what you can remember!"

"You want me... to talk...."

"In the name of the inhabitants of Werst, and to ensure the safety of the village, I order you to talk!"

A nice tall glass of *rakiou*, brought by Jonas, had the effect of returning the use of his tongue to the doctor, and it was in broken phrases that he expressed himself:

"We both left... Nic and me.... Madmen... madmen! It took almost an entire day to cross these cursed forests.... Didn't reach the castle till nightfall.... I'm still shaking from it.... I will tremble from it all my life! Nic wanted to go in! Yes! He wanted to spend the night in the keep... might as well call it the bedroom of Beelzebub!"

Dr. Patak said these things in such a hollow voice that everyone there shivered just from listening to him.

"I didn't agree," he went on, "No... I didn't agree! And what would have happened to him... if I had given in to Nic Deck's wishes? Just thinking about it makes my hair stand on end!"

(If the doctor's hair stood up on his skull, it's because he kept mechanically running his hand through it.)

"So Nic was resigned to camping out on the Plateau of Orgall.... What a night... my friends, what a night! You try and rest, when the spirits don't let you sleep for an hour... no, not even an hour! All of a sudden, monsters of fire appeared in the clouds, real *balaurs*! They rushed onto the plateau to devour us...."

All eyes looked up to the sky to see if some stampede of specters was galloping through it.

"And, a few moments later," the doctor went on, "the bell in the chapel started to ring!"

All ears strained towards the horizon, and more than one person thought he heard distant ringing, so impressed was the audience by the doctor's tale.

"Suddenly," he cried, "terrifying roars filled the space... or rather the howls of wild beasts.... Then a bright light shot forth from the windows of the keep... An infernal flame illumined the entire plateau up to the forest.... Nic Deck and I looked at each other.... Oh! How terrifying the sight was! We were like two corpses... two corpses made to grimace at each other by these pale glimmerings!"

And, to look at Dr. Patak with his convulsed face, his mad eyes, there really was reason to wonder if he weren't truly returning from that other world to which he had already sent a good number of his countrymen!

They had to let him catch his breath, for he was incapable of continuing his tale otherwise. That cost Jonas a second glass of *rakiou*, which seemed to restore to the ex-attendant a part of his reason that the evil spirits had made him lose.

"But tell us, what happened to poor Nic Deck?" asked Master Koltz.

And, not without reason, the *biró* attached great importance to the doctor's reply, since it was the young forester who had been personally targeted by the voice of the spirits in the taproom of the King Mathias.

"This is all that stays in my memory," the doctor replied. "Day had returned... I begged Nic Deck to give up his plans.... But you know him... there's no point in trying to change the mind of such a stubborn man.... He went down into the ditch... and I was forced to follow him, since he dragged me behind him.... In any case, I wasn't aware anymore of what I was doing.... Nic went all the way down beneath the barbican.... He grasped a chain from the drawbridge and hoisted himself up it along the outer wall.... At that instant, an awareness of the situation returned to me.... There was still time to stop the foolhardy—I'll even say sacrilegious!—man.... One last time, I ordered him to come back down, to turn back, to take the path to Werst with me.... 'No!' he shouted.... I wanted to run away.... Yes... my friends... I confess... I wanted to run away, and there isn't one of you who wouldn't have had the same thought in my place! But in vain did I try to get up from the ground.... My feet were stuck there... glued... rooted to the spot.... I tried to tear them away... impossible.... I tried to struggle... useless."

And Dr. Patak mimicked the desperate movements of a man held back by his legs, like a fox caught in a trap.

Then, returning to his tale: "At that moment," he said, "a shout could be heard... and what a shout! It was Nic Deck.... His hands, clutching the chain, had let go, and he fell to the bottom of the ditch, as if he had been struck by an invisible hand!"

The doctor did indeed tell things as they had happened, and his imagination hadn't added anything, disturbed as it was. Just as he had described them, so had the wonders occurred for which the Plateau of Orgall had been the theater during the preceding night.

As to what followed Nic Deck's fall: the forester fainted, and Dr. Patak was incapable of coming to his aid, for his boots were stuck to the ground, and his swollen feet couldn't get out of them.... All of a sudden, the invisible force that bound him was broken.... His legs were free.... He hurried towards his companion, and—an act of courage on his part—he moistened Nic Deck's face with his handkerchief, which he had dipped in the water of the moat.... The forester regained consciousness, but his left arm and part of his body were inert from the terrible jolt he had undergone.... However, with the doctor's aid, he managed to get up, climb back up the other side of the counterscarp, and regain the plateau.... Then he set off again for the village.... After an hour's walk, the pains in his arm and side were so violent that they forced him to stop.... Finally, just when the doctor was getting ready to leave and find help in Werst, Master Koltz, Jonas, and Frik arrived just in time.

As to the young forester, if indeed he had been gravely wounded, Dr. Patak avoided saying so—although he usually displayed a rare confidence, when it was a question of a medical diagnosis.

"If you're sick from natural causes," he contented himself with saying in a dogmatic tone, "that's already serious! But if it's a question of a supernatural illness, which the *Chort* sends into your body, no one but the *Chort* can cure you of it!"

For lack of a diagnosis, this prognosis was scarcely reassuring for Nic Deck. Fortunately, these words were not the words of gospel, and any number of doctors have been mistaken since Hippocrates and Galen made their daily mistakes—and they are superior to Dr. Patak. The young forester was a solid youth; with his vigorous constitution, there was hope he'd come out of it—even without any diabolical intervention—only on condition that he didn't follow too precisely the prescriptions of the former quarantine attendant.

VIII

Such events could not calm the terrors of the inhabitants of Werst. There was nothing more to doubt now; those threats that the "mouth of the shade," as the poet would say, had voiced to the customers at the King Mathias were not unfounded. Nic Deck, struck down in an inexplicable way, had been punished for his disobedience and his boldness. Wasn't that a warning to all those who might be tempted to follow his example? It was strictly forbidden to try to get inside the Castle of the Carpathians: That is what must be concluded from this deplorable attempt. Whoever tried it again would risk his life. If the forester had managed to cross the outer wall, he certainly would never have reappeared in the village.

So terror became more widespread than ever in Werst, even in Vulkan, and very likely in the entire valley of the two Sils as well. People went so far as to talk about leaving the country; already some Gypsy families were migrating rather than staying in the vicinity of the castle. Now that it served as a refuge to supernatural, harmful beings, it was beyond what the public temperament could bear. There was nothing left but to go away to some other region of the land, unless the Hungarian government decided to destroy that unapproachable lair. But was the Castle of the Carpathians capable of being destroyed by the ordinary methods that men had at their command?

During the first week of June, no one ventured outside of the village, not even to see to their agricultural duties. Even the slightest digging might provoke the appearance of a phantom, hidden inside the earth.... And couldn't the plow's blade, hollowing out a furrow, make troupes of witches or *strygia* fly out? And wouldn't the seed of demons sprout wherever wheat grains were sown?

"That's exactly what would happen!" the shepherd Frik said with conviction.

And for his part he took care not to go back up to the pastures of the Sil with his sheep.

So the village was terrorized. Work in the fields was completely neglected. People stayed at home, with their doors and windows shut. Master Koltz didn't know what actions to take to restore confidence to his citizens—a confidence that he himself lacked. Decidedly, the only method would be to go to Kolosvar and request the intervention of the authorities.

And the smoke—would it reappear again at the tip of the keep's chimney? Yes, many times the spyglass showed him just that, in the core of the mist that trailed along the surface of the Plateau of Orgall.

And once night fell, didn't the clouds take on a reddish tint, like the reflection of a fire? Yes, and it looked like fiery wreaths were spiraling over the castle.

And those roars, that had so terrified Dr. Patak, were they spreading through the massifs of the Plesa, bringing great terror to the inhabitants of Werst? Yes, or at least, despite the distance, winds from the southwest carried terrible rumblings that reverberated through the pass.

Moreover, according to these terrified people, it was as if the ground itself were being agitated by underground vibrations, as if an ancient volcano in the chain of Carpathian mountains had come back to life. But perhaps there was a fair amount of exaggeration in what the Werstians thought they saw, heard, and felt. Whatever the case, actual, tangible things had occurred—that was a fact—and there was no way of continuing to live in a country that was so extraordinarily disturbed.

It goes without saying that the King Mathias inn continued to be deserted. A lazaretto during an epidemic would not have been more shunned. No one had the audacity to cross the inn's threshold, and Jonas was beginning to wonder if, for lack of customers, he might be reduced to closing down his business, when the arrival of two travelers came to change this state of things.

On the evening of June 9, around eight o'clock, the door's latch was lifted from outside; but the door, bolted inside, could not open.

Jonas, who had already gone up to his attic room, hurried down. The hope he had of finding himself face to face with a guest was intermingled with the fear that this guest might be some appalling revenant, to whom he couldn't refuse food and lodging quickly enough.

So Jonas began prudently negotiating through the door, without opening it.

"Who's there?" he asked.

"Two travelers."

"Alive?"

"Quite alive."

"Are you sure?"

"As alive as can be, Innkeeper, but who will soon die of hunger, if you have the cruelty to keep them out."

So Jonas decided to push back the bolts, and two men came into the room.

Their first concern upon entering was to ask for a room each, since they intended to stay in Werst for twenty-four hours.

In the light from his lamp, Jonas examined the newcomers with extreme attentiveness, and he grew convinced that these were indeed human beings he was dealing with. What good luck for the King Mathias!

The younger of these travelers seemed to be about thirty-two years old. Tall of stature, a noble and handsome face, black eyes, dark brown hair, an elegantly trimmed brown beard, physiognomy a little sad but proud: It all betokened a gentleman, and an innkeeper as observant as Jonas couldn't be mistaken about that.

What's more, when he asked what name he should register the two travelers under:

"Count Franz of Telek," replied the young man, "and his soldier Rotzko."

"From what country?"

"From Craiova."

Craiova is one of the main towns in Romania, which adjoins the Transylvanian provinces near the southern part of the chain of Carpathian mountains. So Franz of Telek was Romanian, which Jonas had recognized at first sight.

As for Rotzko, he was in his forties: tall, robust, with a thick moustache, coarse bushy hair; he had a distinctively military bearing. He was even carrying a soldier's knapsack, attached to his shoulders with straps, and a light-looking suitcase that he held in his hand.

That was all the young count's luggage; he traveled as a tourist, usually by foot. That was obvious from his outfit: coat draped over his shoulders, balaclava on his head, tunic tied at the waist by a belt from which the leather sheath of the Wallachian knife hung, gaiters tightly fitting over wide, thick-soled shoes.

These two travelers were none other than the ones the shepherd Frik had met a dozen days previously on the pass, when they had been headed towards Mt. Retyezat. After visiting the countryside up to the edges of the Maros, and after climbing the mountain, they had come to take a little rest in the village of Werst, before they went on to go back up the valley of the two Sils.

"You have some rooms to give us?" asked Franz of Telek.

"Two... three...four... as many as Your Excellency would like," Jonas replied.

"Two will do," said Rotzko; "so long as they're next to each other."

"Would these do?" Jonas replied, opening two doors at the end of the main room.

"Very well," replied Franz of Telek.

As we can see, Jonas had nothing to fear from his new guests. They weren't at all supernatural beings, spirits that had taken on human appearance. No! This gentleman presented himself as one of those characters of distinction whom an innkeeper is always honored to welcome. This was a fortunate circumstance that would make the King Mathias popular once again.

"How far are we from Kolosvar?" asked the young count.

"About fifty miles, if you follow the road that goes by Petrosani and Karlsburg," Jonas replied.

"Is the journey tiring?"

"Very tiring for pedestrians, and, if I may make this observation to Your Excellency, it would seem a rest of several days would be in order...."

"Can we dine?" asked Franz of Telek, cutting the innkeeper's invitations short.

"Half an hour's patience, and I'll have the honor of offering Your Excellency a meal worthy of him...."

"Bread, wine, eggs, and cold meat will do for us tonight."

"I will serve you."

"As soon as possible."

"This very instant."

And Jonas was getting ready to go to the kitchen, when a question stopped him.

"You don't seem to have many people at your inn...?" said Franz of Telek.

"In fact... there's no one here at this moment, Your Excellency."

"Isn't this the time when the people from the countryside come to drink and smoke their pipes?"

"That hour is past... Your Excellency... the fact is, we go to bed at the same time as the animals in the village of Werst."

He would never have wanted to say why the King Mathias had not one single customer.

"Aren't there four or five hundred inhabitants in your village?"

"About that, Your Excellency."

"But we didn't meet a living soul when we came down the main street...."

"That's because... today... is Saturday... the day before Sunday...."

Franz of Telek didn't insist, fortunately for Jonas, who didn't know how to reply anymore. For nothing in the world would he have consented to confess the true state of affairs. The foreigners would learn it only too soon, and who knows if they wouldn't hasten to flee a village that was so rightfully suspect?

If only that voice doesn't start speaking, while they're in the middle of their dinner, thought Jonas, as he set the table in the middle of the room.

A few moments later, the very simple meal the young count had ordered was properly served on a very white tablecloth. Franz of Telek sat down, and Rotzko took the seat opposite him, as they were accustomed to during their travels. Both ate with great appetite; then, once the meal was over, each retired to his room.

Since the young count and Rotzko hadn't exchanged ten words during the meal, Jonas had been completely unable to join their conversation—to his great displeasure. What's more, Franz of Telek seemed to be not very communicative. As for Rotzko, after observing him, the innkeeper realized that he would be able to get nothing out of him concerning his master's family.

So Jonas had to content himself with wishing his guests goodnight. But before climbing back up to his attic, he looked carefully round the big room, listening anxiously for the slightest noises from within and without, and repeating to himself:

"If only that abominable voice doesn't wake them up from their sleep!"

The night passed calmly.

The next day, at daybreak, the news spread that two travelers were staying at the King Mathias, and a number of inhabitants ran up to the front of the inn.

Very tired from their excursion the day before, Franz of Telek and Rotzko were still sleeping. It was hardly likely that they planned to rise before seven or eight o'clock in the morning.

Hence the great impatience of the curious, who nonetheless would not have had the courage to enter the inn so long as the travelers hadn't left their rooms.

Both finally appeared at the stroke of eight o'clock.

Nothing annoying had happened to them. One could see them walking about inside the inn. Then they sat down for their morning breakfast. That continued to seem reassuring.

Moreover, Jonas, standing in the doorway, smiled in a friendly way, inviting his former customers to have confidence in him again. Since the traveler who was honoring the King Mathias with his presence was a gentleman—a Romanian gentleman, if you please, and of one of the oldest Romanian families—what could one fear in such noble company?

In short, Master Koltz, thinking it was his duty to serve as an example, ventured to put in a token appearance.

Around nine o'clock, the *biró* entered, a little hesitant. Almost immediately, he was followed by Magister Hermod, three or four other regulars, and the shepherd Frik. As for Dr. Patak, it had been impossible to convince him to accompany them.

"Set foot again at Jonas's place," he had replied, "never, even if he paid me ten florins a visit!"

It is fitting to make a remark here that is not without a certain importance: If Master Koltz had agreed to return to the King Mathias, it was not with the sole aim of satisfying a feeling of curiosity, or out of a wish to strike up an acquaintance with Count Franz of Telek. No! Financial interest played a notable role in his decision.

In fact, in his capacity as a traveler, the young count was obliged to pay a transit tax for his soldier and himself. And, we have not forgotten, these taxes went directly into the pocket of the leading magistrate of Werst.

So the *biró* came to make his claim in very proper phrases, and Franz of Telek, although a little surprised at the request, hastened to comply with it.

He even invited Master Koltz and the schoolmaster to sit down for a bit at his table. They accepted, unable to refuse such a politely phrased offer.

Jonas hurried to serve various liqueurs, the best from his cellar. Some people from Werst then asked for a round for their count. So there was reason to believe that the former clientele, once they had left today, would not delay in returning to the King Mathias.

After paying the travelers' tax, Franz of Telek wished to know if it produced much revenue.

"Not as much as we'd like, Your Excellency," Master Koltz replied.

"Do foreigners visit this part of Transylvania only rarely?"

"Rarely, indeed," the *biró* replied, "and yet the country deserves to be explored."

"That is my opinion," said the young count. "What I have seen of it certainly seemed worthy of attracting the attention of travelers. From the top of Mt. Retyezat, I much admired the valleys of the Sil, the hamlets you can see in the east, and the cirque of mountains that the massif of the Carpathians forms in the background."

"It is very beautiful, Your Excellency, it is very beautiful," replied Magister Hermod, "and, to complete your excursion, we suggest you make the ascent of Mt. Paring."

"I fear I won't have enough time," Franz of Telek replied.

"A day would suffice."

"No doubt, but I have to go back to Karlsburg, and I count on leaving tomorrow morning."

"What, Your Excellency wouldn't think of leaving us so soon?" Jonas said in his most gracious manner.

And he would not have been upset to see his two guests prolonging their stay at the King Mathias.

"I must," the Count of Telek replied. "In any case, what would be the point of my staying in Werst?"

"Believe me, our village has enough points of interest to be worth a brief stay for a tourist!" Master Koltz observed.

"But it seems to be little visited," replied the young count, "and that's probably because its environs have nothing curious about them...."

"No, nothing curious," said the *biró*, thinking about the castle.

"No... nothing curious...." repeated the schoolmaster.

"Oh! Oh!" the shepherd Frik said, from whom this exclamation escaped involuntarily.

Such stares Master Koltz and the others—especially the innkeeper—shot at him! Was it so urgent to fill a foreigner in on the secrets of the country? Revealing to him what was happening on the Plateau of Orgall, directing his attention to the Castle of the Carpathians, wasn't that the same as wanting to frighten him, and make him want to leave the village? And in the future, what travelers would want to follow the road over the Vulkan Pass to enter Transylvania?

Truly, this shepherd didn't show any more intelligence than the lowest of his sheep.

"Will you be quiet, imbecile, be quiet!" Master Koltz said to him under his breath.

Still, the curiosity of the young count had been awakened. He addressed Frik directly, and asked him what he meant by these interjections.

The shepherd was not a man to back down, and, at bottom, perhaps he thought that Franz of Telek could give some good advice that the village could turn to its advantage.

"I said, 'Oh! Oh!' Your Excellency," he replied, "and I won't deny it."

"Is there some wonder to visit in the environs of

Werst?" the young count went on.

"Some wonder...." replied Master Koltz.

"No! no!" the others all cried out.

And they were already frightened at the thought that a second attempt made to penetrate the castle would not fail to bring on new misfortunes.

Franz of Telek, not without a little surprise, observed these fine men, whose faces were all equally marked with terror, each in its own way.

"What is it, then?" he asked.

"What is it, master?" Rotzko replied. "Well, apparently there is the Castle of the Carpathians."

"The Castle of the Carpathians?"

"Yes! That's the name this shepherd just whispered into my ear."

And, saying this, Rotzko pointed at Frik, who nodded his head without daring to look at the *biró*.

Now a breach had been made in the wall of the private life of the superstitious village, and its entire history soon passed through this breach.

Master Koltz, who had made his decision, wanted to explain the situation to the young count himself, and he told him all about the Castle of the Carpathians.

It goes without saying that Franz of Telek could not hide the astonishment this tale made him feel and the feelings it suggested to him. Although only somewhat educated in matters of science, like other young men of his background who lived in their castles in the hinterlands of Wallachian countrysides, he was a man of good sense. He believed little in apparitions, and readily laughed at legends. A castle haunted by spirits, that would truly arouse his incredulity. In his opinion, what

Master Koltz had just told him contained nothing miraculous, but only some facts that were more or less established, but to which the people of Werst attributed a supernatural origin. The smoke from the keep, the bell ringing vigorously, that could be explained very simply. As for the flashes of light and the roars coming from the enclosure, it was purely an effect of hallucination.

Franz of Telek didn't at all mind saying so, and joking about it, to the great scandal of his listeners.

"But, Your Excellency," Master Koltz said to him, "there is something else."

"Something else—?"

"Yes! It is impossible to penetrate inside the Castle of the Carpathians."

"Really?"

"Our forester and our doctor wanted to cross its walls a few days ago, out of devotion to the village, and they almost paid dearly for their attempt."

"What happened to them?" asked Franz of Telek in a somewhat ironic tone.

Master Koltz recounted the adventures of Nic Deck and Dr. Patak in detail.

"So," said the young count, "when the doctor wanted to get out of the ditch, his feet were stuck so firmly to the ground that he couldn't take one step forward?"

"Neither forward nor backward!" added Magister Hermod.

"That's what he thought, your doctor," replied Franz of Telek, "and so it was fear that spurred him... even down to his spurs!"

"Perhaps, Your Excellency," Master Koltz continued. "But how can you explain the fact that Nic Deck got a terrible shock, when he put his hand on the hinge of the drawbridge?"

"Some kind of mean trick of which he was the victim...."

"So mean, in fact," the *biró* responded, "that he has been in bed since that day...."

"Not in danger of death, I hope?" the young count hastened to ask.

"No... fortunately."

Actually, that was a material fact, an undeniable fact, and Master Koltz awaited the explanation that Franz of Telek would give of it.

Here is what he replied, very lucidly.

"In all I have just heard, there is nothing, I repeat, that isn't very simple. What I don't doubt at all is that the Castle of the Carpathians is now occupied. By whom? ... I don't know. In any case, they are not spirits, they are people who want to remain hidden, after they have found refuge there... no doubt evildoers...."

"Evildoers?" cried Master Koltz.

"Probably, and since they don't want anyone to come there and expel them, they have tried to make people believe the castle is haunted by supernatural beings."

"What, Your Excellency," replied Magister Hermod, "do you really think...."

"What I think is that this country is very superstitious, and the people in the castle know this, and in this way they want to prevent intruders from visiting."

It was likely enough that things had happened in just this way; but you will not be surprised that no one in Werst wanted to admit this explanation.

The young count saw clearly that he had not in the

least convinced an audience that did not want to let itself be convinced. So he confined himself to adding: "Since you do not care to agree with my explanations, gentlemen, continue to believe whatever you like about the Castle of the Carpathians."

"We believe what we have seen, Your Excellency," replied Master Koltz.

"And what exists," the schoolmaster added.

"Perhaps, and, really, I regret I don't have twenty-four hours at my disposal, since Rotzko and I would have gone to visit your famous castle, and I assure you we would soon have found out what we were dealing with...."

"Visit the castle!" cried Master Koltz.

"Without the least hesitation, and the devil in person would not have prevented us from entering the enceinte."

Hearing Franz of Telek express himself in such positive terms, even such mocking ones, everyone there was seized with a very different sort of terror. Wouldn't treating the spirits of the castle with such nonchalance attract some catastrophe to the village? Didn't these demons hear everything that was said at the inn of the King Mathias? ... Wasn't the voice going to ring out a second time?

And, speaking about that matter, Master Koltz told the young count the story of how the forester had been threatened by his own name with a terrible punishment, if he decided to try to discover the castle's secrets.

Franz of Telek contented himself with shrugging his shoulders; then he got up, saying that no voice could ever have been heard in that room, as they claimed. All of that, he asserted, existed only in the imagination of the over-credulous customers at the inn, a little too fond of schnapps.

At that, some of those present headed for the door, hardly venturing to stay any longer in a place where this young skeptic dared to state such things.

Franz of Telek stopped them with a gesture.

"Decidedly, gentlemen," he said, "I see that the village of Werst is in the grip of fear."

"And with reason, Your Excellency," replied Master Koltz.

"Well, the way to get rid of the machinations that, according to you, are occurring at the Castle of the Carpathians is very clear. The day after tomorrow, I will be in Karlsburg, and, if you like, I will notify the city authorities. They will send you a squad of gendarmes or policemen, and I tell you that these brave men will know perfectly well how to penetrate the castle, either to chase out the pranksters who are toying with your credulity, or to arrest the malefactors who might be preparing some evil deed."

Nothing was more acceptable than this proposition, and yet it was not to the liking of the leading inhabitants of Werst. According to them, neither gendarmes, nor police, nor the army itself could get the better of these superhuman beings, ready to defend themselves with supernatural methods.

"But I think, gentlemen," the young count continued, "that you haven't yet told me to whom the Castle of the Carpathians belongs, or used to belong?"

"To an ancient family from this country, the family of the barons of Gortz," replied Master Koltz.

"The family of Gortz?" cried Franz of Telek.

"The very one!"

"The family that Baron Rudolf belonged to...?"

"Yes, Your Excellency."

"And do you know what has become of him?"

"No. It's been a number of years now since the Baron of Gortz last appeared at the castle."

Franz of Telek had grown pale, and, mechanically, he kept repeating this name in a changed voice:

"Rudolf of Gortz!"

IX

The family of the Counts of Telek, one of the most ancient and illustrious in Romania, already held a considerable rank before the country acquired its independence around the beginning of the sixteenth century. Associated with all the political events that shaped the history of these provinces, the name of this family is gloriously inscribed in that history.

At present, less favored than that famous beech tree at the Castle of the Carpathians on which three branches remained, the house of Telek was reduced to one alone, the branch of the Teleks of Craiova, of which this young gentleman who had just arrived in the village of Werst was the last offshoot.

During his childhood, Franz had never left the patrimonial castle, where the Count and Countess of Telek resided. The descendants of this family enjoyed great consideration, and they put their fortune to good use. Leading the life of ease and pleasure of the nobility of the countryside, they hardly left the Craiova residence more than once a year when their affairs summoned them to the hamlet of that name, even though it was only a few miles away.

This kind of existence necessarily influenced the education of their only son, and Franz must for a long time have felt the effects of the environment where his youth was spent. For a tutor he had only an old Italian priest, who could teach him nothing but what he himself knew, and he didn't know much. Thus the child, having become a young man, had acquired a very scanty knowledge of the sciences, the arts, and contemporary literature. Hunting with passion, running through the forests and plains night and day, pursuing deer or wild boar, attacking, knife in hand, the wild beasts of the mountains—those were the usual pastimes of the young count, who, being very brave and very resolute, accomplished veritable feats of prowess in these rough exercises.

The Countess of Telek died when her son was scarcely fifteen years of age, and he hadn't yet reached twenty-one when the Count perished in a hunting accident.

The grief suffered by young Franz was extreme. Just as he mourned his mother, he mourned his father. Both had been snatched from him in the span of just a few years. All his tenderness, all the affection his heart contained, had till then been concentrated in filial love, which can be enough for the expansions of childhood and adolescence. But when the objects of this love were missing, never having had any friends, and his preceptor too being dead, he found himself alone in the world.

The young count stayed for three more years at the castle of Craiova, which he no longer wanted to leave. He lived there without seeking to create any outside relationships. He went only once or twice to Bucharest, since certain business affairs forced him to. But these were only brief absences, for he was always eager to return to his home.

This existence, however, could not last forever, and Franz ended up feeling a need to widen a horizon that the Romanian mountains narrowly limited, and to soar beyond them.

The young count was about twenty-three years old when he resolved to travel. His wealth would allow him easily to satisfy his new tastes. One day he left the castle of Craiova to the care of his old servants and left the Wallachian country. He brought with him Rotzko, a former Romanian soldier, who had already been in the service of the family of Telek for ten years, as companion of all his hunting expeditions. He was a man of courage and resolution, entirely devoted to his master.

The young count's intention was to visit Europe, staying for a few months in the major capitals and cities of the continent. He thought—not without reason— that his instruction, which had only been roughly sketched out at the castle of Craiova, could be completed by the teachings of travel, the itinerary for which he had carefully prepared.

Franz of Telek wanted to visit Italy first of all, since he spoke Italian (which the old priest had taught him) quite fluently. The attraction of this land, so rich in memories, towards which he felt favorably drawn, was such that he stayed there for four years. He left Venice only to go to Florence, Rome to go to Naples, continually returning to these artistic centers, from which he could not tear himself away. France, Germany, Spain, Russia, England—he would see them later on, would even, he thought, study them more profitably when age had matured his ideas. To taste the charms of the great Italian cities, though, one needed all the effervescence of youth.

Franz of Telek was twenty-seven years old when he went to Naples for the last time. He counted on spending just a few days there before returning to Sicily. He wanted to end his journey exploring the old *Trinacria*; then he would return to the castle of Craiova and rest there for a year.

An unexpected circumstance would not only change his plans, but decide his life and modify its course.

During these few years lived in Italy, though the young count had advanced little in matters of science for which he felt no aptitude, at least the sentiment of beauty had been revealed to him, as light is revealed to a man who had been blind. His mind was generously opened to the masterpieces of painting when he visited the museums of Naples, Venice, Rome, and Florence. At the same time, the theaters had introduced him to the lyric works of that era, and he had come to love the interpretation of the great actors.

It was during his last stay in Naples, and under peculiar circumstances that will be related, that a sentiment of a more intimate nature, and of a more intense penetration, took over his heart.

There was in that time at the Theater of San Carlo a famous singer, whose pure voice, accomplished technique, and dramatic skill aroused the admiration of the dilettanti. Until then La Stilla had never sought the applause of foreign lands, and she sang no other music than Italian music, which once again had come into fashion as the height of musical art. The Carignan Theater in Turin, La Scala in Milan, La Fenice in Venice, the Alfieri theater in Florence, the Apollo theater in Rome, San Carlo in Naples, all hosted her in turn, and her triumphs left her with no regret that she had not yet appeared on the other stages of Europe.

La Stilla, who was then twenty-five, was a woman of incomparable beauty, with her long gold-tinged hair, her deep black eyes, where flames sparkled, the purity of her features, her warm complexion, her waist that the chisel of a Praxiteles could not have made more perfect. And from this woman a sublime artist emerged, another Malibran, about whom Musset also said:

> And your songs in the heavens
> carried away grief!

But this voice, which the most beloved of poets celebrated in his immortal stanzas:

> ...that voice from the heart which
> alone can reach the heart,

that voice, was the voice of La Stilla in all its inexpressible magnificence.

Nevertheless, that great artist who reproduced the accents of tenderness, the most powerful sentiments of the soul, with such perfection—never yet, they said, had her heart felt their effects. Never had she loved, never had her eyes responded to the thousand gazes that enveloped her onstage. It seemed that she wanted to live only in her art and solely for her art.

The first time he saw La Stilla, Franz felt the irresistible impulses of a first love. Immediately renouncing the plan he had formed to leave Italy after visiting Sicily, he resolved to remain in Naples until the end of the season. As if some invisible bond which he did not have the strength to break linked him to the singer, he attended all those performances that the public's enthusiasm turned into veritable triumphs. Many times, incapable of mastering his passion, he had tried to approach her; but La Stilla's door remained pitilessly closed to him as to so many other of her fanatic admirers.

The consequence of this is that the young count was soon the most pitiable of all men. Thinking only of La Stilla, living only to see her and hear her, not seeking to form relationships in society to which his name and fortune summoned him, under that oppression of the heart and mind, his health was soon seriously compromised. And we can only imagine what he would have suffered if he had had a rival. But he knew that no one could thus offend him—not even a certain rather strange individual, whose character and particularities the events of this story require us to expound.

He was a man of about fifty or fifty-five—or so he seemed at the time of Franz of Telek's last journey to Naples. This uncommunicative person seemed to affect to keep himself outside of those social conventions that are expected of the upper classes. No one knew anything about his family, his situation, or his past. He could be seen today in Rome, tomorrow in Florence—depending, that is to say, on whether La Stilla was in Florence or Rome. In reality, only one passion was known to be his: hearing the prima donna of such great renown, who then occupied first place in the art of song.

Though Franz of Telek lived only for La Stilla from the very first day he saw her on the stage in Naples, it was six years now that this eccentric dilettante lived only to hear her, and it seemed that the voice of the singer had become as necessary to his life as the air he breathed. He had never tried to meet her outside of the theater; he had never introduced himself to her or written to her. But every time La Stilla was to sing, at any theater in Italy, one could see at the ticket office a man of tall stature wrapped in a long dark overcoat, wearing a broad-brimmed hat that hid his face. This man hurried to take his place deep in his shuttered loge, which had been rented for him beforehand. He remained shut up in it, motionless and silent, during the entire performance. Then as soon as La Stilla had finished her final aria he furtively slipped away, and no other singer, male or female, could make him stay; he would not even have heard them.

Who was this so persistent spectator? La Stilla had tried in vain to find out. Then, since she was of a very impressionable nature, she had ended up being frightened at the presence of this strange man—an unreasonable fear, though a very real one. Although she could not see him in the back of his loge, the grille of which he never opened, she knew he was there, she could feel his imperious gaze fixed on her, and it disturbed her so much she didn't even hear the bravos with which the audience welcomed her entrance on the stage.

As noted earlier, this person had never introduced himself to La Stilla. But though he had not tried to meet the woman—we will place particular emphasis on this point—anything that might remind him of the artist had been the object of his constant attention. That is why he owned the most beautiful of the portraits that the great painter Michel Gregorio had made of the singer—passionate, vibrant, sublime, incarnating one of her most beautiful roles, and this portrait, which cost its weight in gold, was worth the price her admirer had paid.

Although this odd man was always alone when he came to sit in his box at La Stilla's performances, though he never left his house except to go to the theater, we should not come to the conclusion that he lived in absolute isolation. No, a companion, just as bizarre as he, shared his existence.

This individual was named Orfanik. How old was he, where did he come from, where was he born? No one could have answered these three questions. To hear him talk—and he talked willingly—he was one of those unknown scholars, whose genius had gone unrecognized, and who had grown averse to society. People thought, not without reason, that he must be some poor devil of an inventor generously supported by the purse of the rich dilettante.

Orfanik was of average size, thin, sickly, bony, with one of those pale faces that in the old days would have been described as "whey-faced." As his trademark feature he wore a black eye patch over his right eye, which he must have lost in some experiment in physics or chemistry; on his nose, he wore a pair of thick glasses whose single myopic glass served his left eye, lit up with a greenish gaze. During his solitary walks, he gesticulated, as if he were chatting with some invisible being who listened to him without ever answering.

These two men, the strange music lover and the no less strange Orfanik, were very well known, at least as much as they could be, in these Italian cities, where the theatrical season regularly summoned them. They had the privilege of exciting the curiosity of the public and, although the admirer of La Stilla had always dismissed reporters and their indiscreet interviews, people had finally discovered his name and his nationality. This character was of Romanian origin, and, when Franz of Telek asked what his name was, people replied:

"Baron Rudolf of Gortz."

That's how things stood at the time when the young count had just arrived in Naples. For two months, the Teatro San Carlo was never empty, and the success of La Stilla increased every night. Never had she shown herself as admirable in the various roles of her repertory, never had she provoked more enthusiastic ovations.

At each one of these performances, while Franz sat in his seat in the orchestra, the Baron of Gortz, hidden in the back of his loge, was absorbed in her exquisite arias, soaked up this penetrating voice, without which it seemed he would no longer be able to live.

Then a rumor ran through Naples, a rumor the public refused to believe, but which ended up alarming the world of the dilettanti.

They were saying that, once the season was over, La Stilla was going to renounce the stage. Amazing! In full possession of her talent, in the fullness of her beauty, at

the apogee of her artistic career, was it possible that she
thought of retiring?

As unlikely as this was, it was true, and, without his
suspecting it, the Baron of Gortz was partly the reason for
this resolution.

This spectator with the mysterious aura, always
there, although invisible behind the bars of his loge, had
ended up provoking in La Stilla a nervous and persistent
emotion, from which she could no longer defend herself.
As soon as she came onto the stage, she felt so overwhelmed that this confusion, quite apparent to the public, had little by little altered her health. To leave Naples,
to flee to Rome, to Venice, or to some other city on the
peninsula, would not have been enough, she knew, to
free her from the presence of the Baron of Gortz. She
could not even manage to escape him by leaving Italy for
Germany, Russia, or France. He would follow her wherever she went to sing, and, to free herself from this
haunting importunity, the only solution was to abandon
the operatic stage.

Now, for two months, before the rumor of her retire-
ment had spread, Franz of Telek had decided to take
action with regard to the singer, the consequences of
which would unfortunately lead to the most irreparable
of catastrophes. Unattached, master of a large fortune, he
had contrived to have himself introduced to La Stilla,
and he had offered her the choice of becoming Countess
of Telek.

La Stilla had long known the feelings she inspired in
the young count. She had told herself that he was a gentleman, to whom any woman, even of the highest society, would have willingly entrusted her happiness. Thus,

in the frame of mind she was then, when Franz of Telek offered her his name, she welcomed it with a friendliness she did not in the least try to hide. It was with complete faith in his sentiments that she agreed to become the wife of the Count of Telek, and without any regret at having to abandon her dramatic career.

So the news was true; La Stilla would reappear no more on the stage, as soon as the season at the San Carlo was over. Her marriage, which some people had already suspected, was now reported as definite.

As you can imagine, this produced a prodigious effect, not just among the artistic world, but also in the high society of Italy. After refusing to believe in the realization of this plan, people had to reconcile themselves to it. Jealousies and hatreds sprang up towards the young count, who was stealing away from her art, her successes, the idolatry of the dilettanti, the greatest singer of the time. Thus Franz of Telek began to receive personal threats—threats that the young man didn't worry about for an instant.

But if that was how it was with the public, imagine what Baron Rudolf of Gortz must have felt at the thought that La Stilla was going to be taken away from him, that he would lose with her all that attached him to life. The rumor spread that he tried to end it all with suicide. What is certain is that from that day forward, people stopped seeing Orfanik in the streets of Naples. No longer leaving the side of Baron Rudolf, he came often to enclose himself with him in that loge at the San Carlo that the baron occupied at each performance—which he had never done before, since he had always been absolutely resistant to the charm of music, like so many other scientists.

But as the days went by, emotions did not calm down; they would reach their height on the evening when La Stilla was to make her final appearance on the stage. It was in the superb role of Angelica, in *Orlando*, that masterpiece by Maestro Arconati, that she would say her adieus to the public.

That night, the San Carlo was ten times too small to contain the spectators who jostled each other to get through its doors, and most of whom had to stand outside in the square. People feared shows of violence against the Count of Telek, if not while La Stilla was on stage, then at least after the curtain was lowered on the fifth act of the opera.

The Baron of Gortz had taken his place in the loge, and, once again, Orfanik was next to him.

La Stilla appeared, more agitated than she had ever been. But she recovered herself, abandoned herself to her inspiration, and sang, with such perfection, with such incomparable talent, that it cannot be expressed. The indescribable enthusiasm she excited among the spectators rose to the point of frenzy.

During the performance, the young count had remained in the back of the wings, impatient, nervous, feverish, unable to calm himself, cursing the length of the scenes, getting irritated at the delays caused by the applause and encores. Ah! How impatient he was to take away from this theater the woman who would become the Countess of Telek, take her far, far away, so far away that she would belong to none but him, him alone!

Finally that dramatic scene arrived when the heroine of *Orlando* dies. Never had the admirable music of

Arconati seemed more penetrating, never had La Stilla interpreted it with more passionate accents. Her entire soul seemed to exude from her lips.... And yet it was as if this voice, at times torn apart, would soon break, that voice that would no longer be heard!

At that instant, the bars of the Baron of Gortz's loge were lowered. A strange head, with long graying hair and flaming eyes, showed itself, its ecstatic face terrifying in its pallor, and, from the back of the wings, Franz could see it fully illumined, with a light that had not yet reached him.

La Stilla was letting herself be carried away then by all the fieriness of that uplifting stretto of the final aria.... She had just repeated this phrase with a sublime sentiment:

Innamorata, mio cuore tremante,
Voglio morire....

Suddenly, she stopped....

The face of the Baron of Gortz terrified her.... An inexplicable terror paralyzed her.... She brought her hand quickly to her mouth, which was red with blood.... She tottered.... She fell....

The audience stood up, shaken with emotion, at the height of anguish....

A cry escaped from the loge of the Baron of Gortz....

Franz had just rushed onto the stage; he took La Stilla in his arms, lifted her up... gazed at her... called her name...

"Dead! Dead!" he cried, "Dead!"

La Stilla was dead.... A blood vessel had broken in

her chest... her song was extinguished with her last sigh!

The young count was brought back to his hotel, in such a state that people feared for his reason. He was unable to attend La Stilla's funeral, which was held in the midst of an immense crowd of the Neapolitan populace.

At the cemetery of the Campo Santo Nuovo, where the singer was buried, one can read this name, alone on white marble:

STILLA

The evening of the funeral, a man came to the Campo Santo Nuovo. There, his eyes haggard, his head bowed, his lips clenched as if they had already been sealed by death, he looked for a long time at the place where La Stilla was buried. He seemed to be listening, as if the voice of the great artist could escape one last time from this tomb....

It was Rudolf of Gortz.

That very night, the Baron of Gortz, accompanied by Orfanik, left Naples, and, after his departure, no one knew what became of him.

But, the next day, a letter arrived addressed to the young count.

This letter contained only these words, of a menacing terseness:

"It's you who killed her! Evil will befall you, Count Telek!

RUDOLF OF GORTZ."

X

Such had been the appalling story.

For a month, Franz of Telek's existence was in danger. He could recognize no one—not even his soldier Rotzko. At the height of his fever, one single name would part his lips, which were ready to give up their last breath: It was that of La Stilla.

The young count escaped death. Due to the skill of the doctors, the tireless care of Rotzko, and also with the help of youth and nature, Franz of Telek was saved. His reason emerged intact from that frightening shock. But, when his memory returned to him, when he remembered the tragic final scene of *Orlando*, in which the artist's soul had been broken: "Stilla…! My Stilla!" he would cry out, while his hands were poised as if to applaud her again.

As soon as his master could leave his bed, Rotzko got

him to agree to flee this cursed city, and to let himself be transported to his castle in Craiova. Still, before abandoning Naples, the young count wanted to go and pray at the dead woman's tomb, and give her one final, eternal farewell.

Rotzko accompanied him to the Campo Santo Nuovo. Franz threw himself on that cruel earth, tried to dig it up with his nails, to bury himself in it.... Rotzko managed to drag him far from the tomb, where all his happiness lay.

A few days later, Franz of Telek, back in Craiova, deep in the Wallachian countryside, had seen again the ancient home of his family. He lived inside this castle for five years in total isolation, from which he refused to emerge. Neither time nor distance had been able to bring him any lessening of his suffering. He would have had to forget her, and that was out of the question. The memory of La Stilla, lively as on the first day, was part and parcel of his existence. There are wounds that only death can heal.

Now, at the time when this story begins, the young count had left the castle a few weeks before. Such protracted and urgent appeals Rotzko had to utter to make his master decide to break with that solitude where he was withering away! Franz could not manage to console himself, but at least it was necessary that he try to distract himself from his suffering.

Plans for a long journey had been postponed, so they could first visit the Transylvanian provinces. Later on— Rotzko hoped—the young count would consent to resume that journey through Europe that had been interrupted by the sad events in Naples.

Franz of Telek had left, then, as a tourist this time, and only for a brief exploration. Rotzko and he had climbed the Wallachian plains up to the imposing massif of the Carpathians; they had entered the gorges of the Vulkan Pass; then, after the ascent of Mt. Retyezat and an excursion through the valley of the Maros, they had come to rest at the village of Werst, at the King Mathias inn.

We know what the state of people's minds was when Franz of Telek arrived, and how he had been informed of the incomprehensible facts of which the castle was the theater. We know too how he had just learned that the castle belonged to the Baron Rudolf of Gortz.

The effect produced by this name on the young count had been too marked for Master Koltz and the other noteworthy citizens not to notice it. Rotzko wished this Master Koltz would go to the devil, since he had so inopportunely uttered it, along with his stupid stories. What a bad piece of luck, to have brought Franz of Telek precisely to this village of Werst, in the vicinity of the Castle of the Carpathians!

The young count remained silent. His gaze, wandering from one to the other, showed only too plainly the profound disturbance of his soul, which he was vainly trying to calm.

Master Koltz and his friends understood that a mysterious link must attach the Count of Telek to the Baron of Gortz but, curious as they were, they confined themselves to proper discretion and did not try to learn more. Later on, they would see what could be done.

A few moments later, they had all left the King Mathias, very much intrigued by this extraordinary chain of adventures, which foretold nothing good for the village.

Further, now that the young Count knew to whom the Castle of the Carpathians belonged, would he keep his promise? Once he had arrived in Karlsburg, would he tell the authorities and ask for their intervention? That is what the *biró*, the schoolmaster, Dr. Patak, and others were wondering. In any case, if he didn't do so, Master Koltz had decided to do it himself. The police would be told, they would come visit the castle, and they would see if it was haunted by spirits or inhabited by criminals, for the village could not remain any longer in the grip of such an obsession.

For most of the inhabitants, it is true, that was a useless attempt, a vain endeavor. Launch an attack on demons! ...The policemen's swords would break like glass, and their rifles misfire every shot!

Franz of Telek, who had remained in the main room of the King Mathias alone, abandoned himself to the flow of those memories that the name of Baron Gortz had just so painfully recalled.

After staying for an hour as if annihilated in a chair, he got up, left the inn, headed for the end of the terrace, and looked into the distance.

On the hilltop of the Plesa, in the center of the Plateau of Orgall, stood the Castle of the Carpathians. There this strange character had lived, the spectator at the San Carlo, the man who inspired such an insurmountable terror in the unfortunate Stilla. But, now the castle was abandoned, and Baron Gortz hadn't returned there since the time he fled Naples. No one even knew what had become of him, and it was possible that he had put an end to his existence, after the death of the great artist.

Franz wandered from one hypothesis to another, not knowing before which one to come to rest.

Moreover, the adventure of the forester Nic Deck continued to preoccupy him to a certain degree, and he would have liked to discover its mystery, even if only to reassure the population of Werst.

Thus, since the young count did not doubt that criminals had taken the castle as a hideout, he resolved to keep the promise he had made to thwart the tricks of these fake phantoms, by telling the police at Karlsburg.

Still, to be able to take action, Franz wanted to have more specific details about this affair. The best thing was to go to the young forester in person. That is why, around three o'clock in the afternoon, before returning to the King Mathias, he presented himself at the *biró*'s house.

Master Koltz was very honored to receive him—a gentleman such as the Count of Telek... this descendant of a noble family of Romanian race... to whom the village of Werst would be indebted for finding peace again... and also prosperity... since the tourists would return to visit the country... and to pay the traveling fees, without having anything to fear from the demons of the Castle of the Carpathians... and so on.

Franz of Telek thanked Master Koltz for his compliments, and asked if there would be any danger if he were introduced to Nic Deck.

"None whatsoever, Your Excellency," replied the *biró*. "This brave boy is doing as well as possible, and it will not be long before he resumes his duties."

Then, turning around:

"Isn't that true, Miriota?" he added, talking to his daughter, who had just entered the room.

"By God's grace, father!" Miriota replied in a trembling voice.

Franz was charmed by the gracious greeting the young woman addressed to him. And, seeing that she was still anxious about the state of her fiancé, he hastened to ask her for some explanations on the subject.

"According to what I have heard," he said, "Nic Deck was not gravely wounded...."

"No, Your Excellency," Miriota replied, "and Heaven be praised for that!"

"Do you have a good doctor in Werst?"

"Hmm!" Master Koltz said, in a tone that was scarcely flattering for the former quarantine attendant.

"We have Dr. Patak," replied Miriota.

"The same one who accompanied Nic Deck to the Castle of the Carpathians?"

"Yes, Your Excellency."

"Miss Miriota," Franz said then, "I would like to see your fiancé, in his own interest, and to obtain more precise details about this adventure."

"He would be eager to give them to you, even at the cost of a little fatigue...."

"Oh! I won't take advantage of him, Miss Miriota, and I won't do anything that might harm Nic Deck."

"I know, Your Excellency."

"When will your wedding take place?"

"In about two weeks," replied the *biró*.

"Then I will have the pleasure of attending it, if Master Koltz should still wish to invite me...."

"Your Excellency, such an honor...."

"In a few weeks, then, it's agreed: And I am certain that Nic Deck will be cured, as soon as he can allow himself a little walk with his pretty fiancée."

"May God protect him, Your Excellency!" the young woman replied, blushing.

And, at that moment, her charming face expressed such a visible anxiety, that Franz asked her the reason.

"Yes! May God protect him," Miriota replied, "for, by trying to penetrate the castle despite their defenses, Nic braved malevolent spirits! ...And who knows if they won't persist in trying to torment him all his life...."

"Oh! As to that, Miss Miriota," Franz replied, "we'll set things right, I promise."

"Nothing will happen to my poor Nic?"

"Nothing, and thanks to the agents of the police, in a few days we'll be able to walk through the castle's walls with as much safety as the square in Werst!"

The young count, deeming it ill-timed to discuss this question of the supernatural with people of such prejudiced minds, asked Miriota to take him to the forester's room.

This the young woman hastened to do, and she left Franz alone with her fiancé.

Nic Deck had been told about the arrival of the two travelers at the King Mathias inn. Seated deep within an old armchair wide as a sentry box, he got up to welcome his visitor. Since he now felt almost none of the paralysis that had temporarily struck him, he was well enough to answer the Count of Telek's questions.

"Mr. Deck," Franz said, after shaking the young forester's hand in a friendly way, "I will ask you first of all: Do you believe in the presence of supernatural beings in the Castle of the Carpathians?"

"I am forced to believe so, Your Excellency," Nic Deck replied.

"And they are what prevented you from entering the enclosure?"

"I am certain of it."

"Why is that, would you tell me?"

"Because, if there were no spirits, what happened to me would be inexplicable."

"Would you be so kind as to tell me what happened, omitting nothing?"

"Willingly, Your Excellency."

Nic Deck recounted the story that was requested of him in minute detail. It could only confirm the facts that had been related to Franz during his conversation with the customers at the King Mathias—facts to which the young count, as we know, gave a purely natural interpretation.

In brief, the events of that night of adventures could all be easily explained if the human beings, evildoers or not, who occupied the castle, possessed the machinery capable of producing these phantasmagorical effects. As to that singular claim of Dr. Patak that he had felt chained to the ground by some invisible force, one could argue that said doctor had been the dupe of an illusion. What seemed likely was that his legs had failed him quite simply because he was mad with terror, and this is what Franz said to the young forester.

"How is it, Your Excellency," Nic Deck replied, "that the instant he wanted to run away, his legs failed the coward? That is hardly possible, you'll agree...."

"Well then," Franz continued, "let us agree that his

feet were caught in some hidden trap beneath the weeds at the bottom of the ditch...."

"When traps close," the forester replied, "they wound you cruelly; they tear your flesh, and Dr. Patak's legs have no trace of a wound."

"Your observation is true, Nic Deck, and yet, believe me, if it is true that the doctor was unable to free himself, that's because his feet were held back in that way...."

"Then I will ask you, Your Excellency, how could a trap open back up by itself and set the doctor free again?"

Franz was somewhat at a loss as to how to respond.

"But, Your Excellency," the forester went on, "I leave to you the things having to do with Dr. Patak. After all, I can only assert what I know for myself."

"Yes... let's put aside this fine doctor, and talk only about what happened to you, Nic Deck."

"What happened to me is very clear. There is no doubt that I received a terrible shock, and that in a way that is hardly natural."

"There is no appearance of a wound on your body?" Franz asked.

"None, Your Excellency, and yet I was struck with such violence...."

"Was it precisely at the moment you placed your hand on the hinge of the drawbridge?"

"Yes, Your Excellency, and scarcely had I touched it when I was as if paralyzed. Fortunately, my other hand, which was holding onto the chain, did not let go, and I slipped to the bottom of the ditch, where the doctor lifted me up unconscious."

Franz shook his head like a man whom these explanations left incredulous.

"Look, Your Excellency," Nic Deck continued, "what I told you just now, I did not dream, and since, for eight days, I've stayed stretched out on this bed, not having the use of either my arm or my leg, it's not reasonable to say I imagined all that!"

"But I do not claim that, and it is quite certain you received a brutal shock...."

"Brutal and diabolical!"

"No, and that's where we differ, Nic Deck," the young count replied. "You think you were struck by a supernatural being, but I do not think so, because supernatural beings do not exist—neither harmful ones nor beneficial ones."

"So then, Your Excellency, would you please give me the explanation for what happened to me?"

"I cannot yet, Nic Deck, but be sure that everything will be explained, and in the simplest way."

"Please God!" the forester replied.

"Tell me," Franz continued, "has this castle always belonged to the family of Gortz?"

"Yes, Your Excellency, and it still belongs to it, although the last descendant of the family, Baron Rudolf, has disappeared without anyone hearing any news about him."

"And how long ago did this disappearance occur?"

"It happened about twenty years ago."

"Twenty years ago?"

"Yes, Your Excellency. One day, Baron Rudolf left the castle; the last servant there passed away a few months after his departure, and we haven't seen him since."

"And since then, no one has set foot in the castle?"

"No one."

"And what do they think hereabouts?"

"They think Baron Rudolf must have died abroad, and that his death occurred soon after his disappearance."

"They are mistaken, Nic Deck, and the baron was still alive—at least he was five years ago."

"He was alive, Your Excellency?"

"Yes... in Italy... in Naples."

"You saw him?"

"I saw him."

"And after five years ago...?"

"I haven't heard any more talk of him."

The young forester remained pensive. An idea had come to him—an idea he was hesitant to express. Finally he made up his mind, and raising his head, with knitted brows:

"It is not likely, Your Excellency," he said, "is it, that Baron Rudolf of Gortz came back to our country with the intention of locking himself up in the depths of this castle...?"

"No... that is not likely, Nic Deck."

"What would his interest be in hiding himself there... in letting no one reach him there?"

"None," replied Franz of Telek.

And yet, that was a thought that was beginning to take shape in the young count's mind. Wasn't it possible that this character, whose existence had always been so enigmatic, had come to take refuge in this castle, after his departure from Naples? Here, thanks to superstitious beliefs cleverly maintained, wouldn't it be easy for him, if he wanted to live in absolute isolation, to defend himself against any irksome inquisitiveness, since it was a given that he knew the state of mind of the people in the surrounding countryside?

Still, Franz thought it useless to have the inhabitants of Werst entertain this hypothesis. And he would have had to tell them about facts that were too personal to him. Moreover, he would not have convinced anyone, and he knew this clearly, when Nic Deck added:

"If it is the Baron Rudolf who is at the castle, we'd have to believe that Baron Rudolf is the *Chort*, for only the *Chort* could have treated me that way!"

Not wanting to go back over that again, Franz changed the course of the conversation. When he had used all means possible to reassure the forester on the consequences of his attempt, he made him promise, however, not to try it again. It was not his affair, but a matter for the authorities, and the agents of the Karlsburg police would certainly know how to penetrate the mystery of the Castle of the Carpathians.

The young count then took leave of Nic Deck, with wishes that he get better as soon as possible so as not to delay his wedding with the pretty Miriota, which he promised to attend.

Absorbed in his thoughts, Franz returned to the King Mathias, from which he did not emerge for the rest of the day.

At six o'clock, Jonas served him dinner in the main room, where, out of a laudable sense of reserve, neither Master Koltz nor anyone in the village came to trouble his solitude.

Around eight o'clock, Rotzko said to the young count:

"You don't need me anymore, master?"

"No, Rotzko."

"Then I'll go smoke my pipe on the terrace."

"Go, Rotzko, go."

Half lying in an armchair, Franz let himself once again go back over the unforgettable course of past events. He was in Naples during the final performance at the Teatro San Carlo.... He could see the Baron of Gortz again, at the instant that man had appeared to him, his head outside of the loge, his gaze ardently fixed on the artist, as if he had wanted to mesmerize her....

Then, the young count's thoughts turned to that letter signed by the strange character, who accused him, Franz of Telek, of having killed La Stilla....

Lost thus in his memories, Franz felt sleep little by little overcoming him. But he was still in that in-between state when one can perceive the slightest noise, when a surprising phenomenon occurred.

It seemed that a voice, sweet and well-modulated, passed through that room where Franz was alone, quite alone.

Without wondering if he was dreaming or not, Franz rose and listened.

Yes! It was as if a mouth had come close to his ear, and invisible lips were uttering Stefano's expressive melody, inspired by these words:

Nel giardino de' mille fiori,
Andiamo, mio cuore...

Franz knew this ballad.... La Stilla had sung it, with an ineffable sweetness, in the recital she had given at the

Teatro San Carlo before her farewell performance....

As if being rocked to a lullaby, without realizing it Franz abandoned himself to the charm of hearing her once again....

Then the phrase came to an end, and the voice, which diminished by degrees, was extinguished in soft vibrations in the air.

But Franz shook off his torpor.... He got up swiftly.... He held his breath, tried to grasp some distant echo of that voice that went to his heart....

Everything was silent, inside and outside.

"Her voice!" her murmured. "Yes! It was truly her voice... the voice of her I loved so much!"

Then, returning to a sense of reality:

"I was sleeping... I dreamed it!" he said.

XI

The next day, the young count woke at dawn, his mind still agitated by the visions of the previous night.

It was the morning that he was supposed to leave the village of Werst to take the road to Kolosvar.

After visiting the industrial hamlets of Petrosani and Livadzel, Franz's intention was to pause for a whole day in Karlsburg, before going to stay for a time in the capital of Transylvania. From there, the train would take him through the provinces of central Hungary, the final stage in his journey.

Franz had left the inn and, as he walked about on the terrace, he looked through his opera glasses and examined with profound emotion the shape of the castle, which the rising sun outlined quite clearly on the Plateau of Orgall.

And his thoughts centered on this point: Once he had

arrived in Karlsburg, would he keep the promise he had made to the people of Werst? Would he tell the police about what was happening at the Castle of the Carpathians?

When the young count had undertaken to restore peace to the village, it was with the private conviction that the castle was serving as a refuge to a band of evil-doers, or, at the very least, to suspicious people who, not wanting to be sought out, had contrived to prohibit any approach.

But, during the night, Franz had reflected. He had undergone a change of mind, and now he was hesitant.

In fact, for five years, the last descendant of the family of Gortz, Baron Rudolf, had disappeared, and no one had ever been able to find out what had become of him. True, the rumor had spread that he had died some time after his departure from Naples. But was there any truth in it? What proof did anyone have of his death? Perhaps Baron Gortz was still alive, and, if he was alive, why shouldn't he have returned to his ancestral castle? Why wouldn't Orfanik, the only companion he was known to have, have accompanied him, and why couldn't that strange physician be the author and director of these phenomena that continued to inspire terror in the country? These were precisely the subjects of Franz's reflections.

One must admit that this hypothesis seemed plausible enough, and, if Baron Rudolf of Gortz and Orfanik had sought refuge in the castle, one could understand why they had wanted to make it unapproachable, so they could lead the life of isolation there that suited their habits and their characters.

But if that's how it was, what line of action should the young count adopt? Was it right for him to seek to intervene in the private affairs of Baron Gortz? That is what he was pondering, weighing the pros and cons of the question, when Rotzko came to join him on the terrace.

He thought it right to disclose to him his ideas about this matter.

"Master," Rotzko replied, "it is possible that it is Baron Gortz who is abandoning himself to these diabolical phantasmagorias. Well, if that is the case, my advice is that we should not get mixed up in it. The cowards of Werst will escape from it as they like, that's their business, and we need not have to worry about returning peace to this village."

"So be it," Franz replied, "and, all things considered, I think you are right, my brave Rotzko."

"I think so too," the soldier simply replied.

"As to Master Koltz and the others, they know how to go about things now, to be rid of the so-called spirits of the castle."

"In fact, master, all they have to do is to tell the Karlsburg police."

"We will set out on our way after lunch, Rotzko."

"Everything will be ready."

"But, before we go back down into the valley of the Sil, we will make a detour towards the Plesa."

"Why is that, master?"

"I'd like to see that singular Castle of the Carpathians up close."

"For what purpose?"

"A whim, Rotzko, a whim that won't delay us even half a day."

Rotzko was distressed by this decision, which seemed to him useless at best. Whatever could remind the young count too vividly of the past, he wanted to banish. This time, his attempts were in vain, and he came up against the inflexible resolution in his master.

This is because Franz—as if he had undergone some kind of irresistible influence—felt himself attracted to the castle. Without his realizing it, perhaps this attraction was linked to that dream in which he had heard the voice of La Stilla murmuring Stefano's plaintive melody.

But had he dreamed it? Yes! That is exactly what he wondered, remembering that, in that very room at the King Mathias, a voice had already made itself heard, they assured him—that voice whose threats Nic Deck had so imprudently braved. Thus, with the count's present state of mind, we should not be surprised that he had formed the plan to head for the Castle of the Carpathians and to climb up to the foot of its old walls—without the intention, however, of penetrating them.

It goes without saying that Franz of Telek had made up his mind not to tell the inhabitants of Werst his intentions. These people would have been capable of uniting with Rotzko to try to dissuade him from approaching the castle, and he had commanded his soldier to keep silence on this plan. Seeing him descend from the village towards the valley of the Sil, no one would doubt that this was in order to take the road to Karlsburg. But, from the top of the terrace, he had noticed that another path ran along the base of the Retyezat up to the Vulkan Pass. So it would be possible to climb up the hills of the Plesa without passing again through the village, and, consequently, without being seen by Master Koltz or the others.

Around noon, after settling without argument the slightly inflated bill Jonas presented to him along with his best smile, Franz readied himself for departure.

Master Koltz, the pretty Miriota, Magister Hermod, Dr. Patak, the shepherd Frik, and a number of other inhabitants had come to bid him farewell.

The young forester had even been able to leave his room, and one could see clearly that it wouldn't be long before he succeeded in getting back on his feet—all the credit for which the ex-quarantine attendant attributed to himself.

"I offer you my congratulations, Nic Deck," Count Franz said to him, "and your fiancée too."

"We accept with gratitude," the young woman replied, radiating happiness.

"May your journey be a fortunate one, Your Excellency," the forester added.

"Yes... may it be so!" Franz replied, whose forehead had clouded.

"Your Excellency," Master Koltz said, "we beg you not to forget the steps you promised to take in Karlsburg."

"I will not forget, Master Koltz," Franz replied. "But, in case I am delayed in my journey, you know this very simple method of ridding yourself of that disturbing neighbor, and the castle will soon cease to inspire fear in the brave population of Werst."

"That is easy to say...." the schoolmaster muttered.

"And to do," Franz replied. "Before 48 hours have passed, if you wish, the police will have gotten the better of whatever beings are hidden in the castle...."

"Except in the very probable case that they are spirits," the shepherd Frik observed.

"Even in that case," Franz replied with an imperceptible shrug of his shoulders.

"Your Excellency," Dr. Patak said, "if you had accompanied us, Nic Deck and me, you might not talk that way!"

"That would surprise me, Doctor," Franz replied, "even if I had been so strangely held back by my feet in the castle's ditch...."

"By your feet, Your Excellency? You mean by your boots! Unless you're claiming that... in the state of mind... in which I found myself... I... dreamed...."

"I claim nothing, sir," Franz replied, "and I will not try to explain to you what seems so inexplicable to you. But be certain that if the police come to visit the Castle of the Carpathians, their boots, which are used to discipline, will not take root as yours did."

Having said that for the doctor's benefit, the young count received one last time the compliments of the innkeeper of the King Mathias, so honored at having had the honor that the honorable Franz of Telek... and so on. Having saluted Master Koltz, Nic Deck, his fiancée, and all the inhabitants gathered on the square, he made a sign to Rotzko. Then they both went down the road to the pass at a brisk walk.

In less than an hour, Franz and his soldier had reached the right bank of the river, which they climbed by following the southern base of Mt. Retyezat.

Rotzko had resigned himself to saying nothing more to his master—it would have been a lost cause. Used to obeying him as a soldier, if the young count threw himself into some perilous adventure, he could rescue him from it.

After two hours' walk, Franz and Rotzko stopped to rest for a bit.

In that place, the Wallachian Sil, which had so slightly bent to the right, came close to the road by a very marked curve. On the other side, on the bulge of the Plesa, the Plateau of Orgall stood clear, about a league away. So it made sense to leave the Sil, since Franz wanted to cross the pass in order to head for the castle.

Obviously, avoiding going back into Werst, this detour had doubled the distance that separated the castle from the village. Nonetheless, it would still be full daylight when Franz and Rotzko arrived at the summit of the Plateau of Orgall. The young count would then have the time to observe the castle from without. Later they would wait till evening to go back down the road to Werst, so it would be easy for him to follow it with the certainty of being seen by no one in the village. Franz's intention was to go to spend the night in Livadzel, a small hamlet at the confluence of the two Sils, and to resume the road to Karlsburg the next day.

The pause lasted for half an hour. Franz, absorbed in his memories, agitated too at the thought that Baron Gortz had perhaps hidden his existence in the depths of this castle, didn't say a word....

And Rotzko had to exercise great self-control not to say to him:

"It is useless to go any further, master! Let's turn our back on this cursed castle, and leave!"

Both began to follow the *thalweg* of the valley floor. They had first of all to make their way through a pathless jumble of trees. Parts of the ground were deeply furrowed, since, during times of heavy rainfall, the Sil sometimes burst its banks, and its overflow ran in tumultuous torrents over these lands, which it changed into swamps. That made for some difficulties in walking, and consequently a little delay. An hour went by before they could rejoin the road to the Vulkan Pass, which they crossed around five o'clock.

The right side of the Plesa is not bristling with those forests that Nic Deck was able to cross only by clearing a passage with a hatchet; but they still had to deal with difficulties of a different kind. These were masses of fallen rock from the moraine, through which one could not venture without proceeding cautiously: sudden unevenness in the ground; deep rifts; blocks of stone that teetered on their base and stood up like seracs in an alpine region; a confused mass of enormous stones that avalanches had thrown from the top of the mountain—in short, a veritable chaos in all its horror.

To climb up the talus slopes in these conditions required another good hour's worth of very difficult effort. It truly seemed as if the Castle of the Carpathians could have defended itself very well just by the impassability of the ways leading to it. And perhaps Rotzko hoped that so many obstacles would come up that it would be impossible to pass: but such was not to be the case.

Beyond the zone of deep rifts and stone boulders, the first crest of the Plateau of Orgall was finally reached. From this vantage, the castle was outlined more clearly in the midst of that gloomy desert, from which terror had kept the inhabitants of the country away for so many years.

What should be noted is that Franz and Rotzko were going to approach the castle from its side wall, the one facing north. Nic Deck and Dr. Patak had arrived at the eastern wall because by skirting the left side of the Plesa, they had left the Nyad river and the road to the pass to the right. Both directions, in fact, sketched an oblique angle, the vertex of which was defined by the central castle keep. On the north side, moreover, it would have been impossible to penetrate the wall, since not only was there neither barbican nor drawbridge, but the outer wall, following the irregularities of the plateau, rose to quite a great height.

But it mattered little that any access was impossible from that side, since the young count was not thinking of passing through the castle walls.

It was seven-thirty when Franz of Telek and Rotzko stopped at the extreme edge of the Plateau of Orgall. Before them that fierce pile drowned in shadow spread out, its hue mixing with the ancient coloration of the rocks on the Plesa. To the left, the wall made a sharp turn, flanked by the corner bastion. It was there, on the terreplein, above its crenellated parapet, that the beech tree grimaced, whose contorted branches bore witness to the violent gusts from the southwest at this height.

In truth, the shepherd Frik had not been mistaken. Judging from it, the legend gave no more than three years of existence to the old castle of the Barons of Gortz.

Franz, silent, looked at all these constructions, dominated by the squat castle keep in the center. There, surely, beneath that jumbled heap, more vaulted rooms were hidden, vast and echoing, long labyrinthine hallways, oubliettes nestled in the bowels of the earth, such as the fortresses of the ancient Magyars still possessed. No other habitation would have been more suitable than this ancient manor for the last descendant of the family of Gortz to hide himself away in it, in an oblivion whose secret no one could ever know. And the more the young count thought about it, the more attached he was to the idea that Rudolf of Gortz had indeed taken refuge in the isolated ramparts of his Castle of the Carpathians.

Nothing, however, revealed the presence of guests of any kind inside the castle keep. Not one plume of smoke rose from its chimneys, not one sound emerged from its hermetically sealed windows. Nothing—not even a bird-call—disturbed the mystery of the shadowy domain.

For some moments, Franz greedily fed his eyes on this enclosure, which in days gone by used to be filled with the tumult of celebrations and the clash of weapons. But he was silent, so haunted was his mind by overwhelming thoughts, his heart full of memories.

Rotzko, who wanted to leave the young count to himself, had taken care to stand some distance away. He would not allow himself to interrupt him by a single remark. But when the sun began to set behind the massif of the Plesa, and the valley of the two Sils began to fill with shadows, he hesitated no longer.

"Master," he said, "night has fallen.... It will soon be eight o'clock."

Franz did not seem to hear him.

"It is time to go," Rotzko continued, "if we want to be in Livadzel before the inns close."

"Rotzko... in an instant... yes... in an instant.... I'll be with you," Franz replied.

"We will need at least an hour, master, to get back to the road to the pass, and since night will have fallen by then, we won't risk being seen when we cross it."

"A few more minutes," Franz replied, "and we will go back down towards the village."

The young count had not moved from the place where he had stopped when they arrived on the Plateau of Orgall.

"Do not forget, master," Rotzko replied, "that, at night, it will be difficult to find our way between the rocks.... We could scarcely manage it when it was broad daylight.... You will excuse me if I insist...."

"Yes... let's go.... Rotzko... I'll follow you...."

And it seemed that Franz was invincibly restrained before the castle, perhaps by one of those secret presentiments that the heart cannot manage to fathom. Was he, then, bound to the ground, as Dr. Patak said he had been in the ditch, at the foot of the wall? ...No! his legs were not bound by any shackle, any trap.... He could come and go on the surface of the plateau, and if he had wanted to, nothing would have prevented him from walking all round the enceinte, alongside the rim of the counterscarp....

Perhaps that was what he wanted to do?

That is what Rotzko thought, who decided to say one last time:

"Are you coming, master?"

"Yes... yes..." Franz replied.

And he remained motionless.

The Plateau of Orgall was already dark. The widening shadow of the massif, climbing up towards the south, hid all the constructions, whose contours were now only an uncertain silhouette. Soon nothing would be visible of it, if no light shone forth from the narrow windows of the castle keep.

"Master... come, then!" Rotzko repeated.

And Franz was finally going to follow him, when, on the terreplein of the bastion, where the legendary beech tree stood, a vague shape appeared....

Franz stopped, looking at that shape, whose profile slowly became clearer.

It was a woman, her hair flowing loose, her hands stretched out, enveloped in a long white dress.

But wasn't this the costume La Stilla wore in that final scene of *Orlando*, where Franz of Telek had seen her for the last time?

Yes! And it was La Stilla, motionless, her arms stretched out to the young count, her penetrating gaze fixed on him....

"It is she! ...It is she!" he cried.

And, rushing forward, he would have run up to the base of the wall, if Rotzko hadn't held him back....

The apparition suddenly disappeared. La Stilla showed herself for scarcely a minute....

It didn't matter! A second would have been enough for Franz to recognize her, and these words escaped him:

"She... she... alive!"

XII

Was it possible? La Stilla—Franz of Telek thought he would never see her again, and she had just appeared to him on the walkway atop the bastion! ...He had not been the victim of an illusion, and Rotzko too had seen her, just as he had! ...It was indeed the great artist, dressed in her Angelica costume, just as she had shown herself to the audience at her farewell performance at the Teatro San Carlo!

The terrifying truth burst open before the young count's eyes. This woman he so loved, the woman who was supposed to have become the Countess of Telek— she had been locked up for five years in the midst of the Transylvanian mountains! The woman whom Franz had seen fall dead on the stage had survived! While they were carrying him dying back to his hotel, Baron Rudolf of Gortz could have penetrated into La Stilla's house, kidnapped her, and dragged her into this Castle of the Carpathians— and it was just an empty coffin that the whole populace had followed the next day to the Campo Santo Nuovo in Naples!

All that seemed incredible, inadmissible, abhorrent to common sense. It was astounding, implausible, and Franz would repeat this over and over again to the point of redundancy.... Yes! But one fact stood out: La Stilla must have been kidnapped by Baron Gortz, since she was in the castle! ... She was alive, since he had just seen her above this wall! ... That was an absolute certainty.

The young count kept trying to recover from the confusion of his thoughts, which soon condensed into one single idea: To tear La Stilla away from Rudolf of Gortz, she who had been a prisoner for five years in the Castle of the Carpathians!

"Rotzko," Franz said in a breathless voice, "listen to me... try to understand me, especially... for it seems to me that rationality is deserting me...."

"Master... my dear master!"

"At all costs, I have to reach her... her! This very night...."

"No... tomorrow...."

"Tonight, I tell you! She is there.... She saw me as I saw her.... She is waiting for me...."

"Well then... I will follow you...."

"No! I will go alone."

"Alone?"

"Yes."

"But how could you enter the castle, if Nic Deck couldn't?"

"I will enter it, I tell you."

"The gate is closed...."

"It will not be closed for me.... I will search.... I will find an opening.... I will go through...."

"Don't you want me to go with you... master... don't you want that?"

"No! We will separate, and it's by our separating that you will be able to help me...."

"So I will wait for you here...?"

"No, Rotzko."

"Where should I go, then?"

"To Werst... or rather... no... not to Werst...." Franz replied. "Those people shouldn't know... Go down to the village of Vulkan, where you'll spend the night... If you don't see me the next day, leave Vulkan in the morning... that is... no... wait there a few more hours.... Then, leave for Karlsburg.... There, you will tell the chief of police.... You will tell him everything.... Finally, return with policemen.... If you have to, storm the castle! Free her! Ah! God in heaven... she's alive... in the power of Rudolf of Gortz!"

And, as these disconnected phrases were being uttered by the young count, Rotzko could see that his master's overexcitement was increasing and revealing itself as the confused emotions of a man who was no longer in full possession of his faculties.

"Go... Rotzko!" he shouted one last time.

"Is that what you really want?"

"Yes!"

Faced with this formal order, Rotzko could do nothing but obey. And Franz had already started to walk away, and already the darkness hid him from the soldier's eyes.

Rotzko remained for a few moments in the same

place, unable to make up his mind to leave. Then the idea came to him that Franz's efforts would be useless, that he would not even manage to get through the wall, that he would be forced to return to the village of Vulkan... perhaps the next day... perhaps this very night.... Both of them could go then to Karlsburg, and what neither Franz nor the forester had been able to do, they would accomplish with the police.... They would get the better of that Rudolf of Gortz.... They would snatch the unfortunate Stilla away from him ....They would dig up that Castle of the Carpathians.... They wouldn't leave behind a stone, if necessary... even if all the devils in hell were gathered together to defend it!

And Rotzko went back down the slopes of the Plateau of Orgall, in order to return to the road to the Vulkan Pass.

Meantime, by following the rim of the counterscarp, Franz had already gone round the corner bastion that flanked it to the left.

A thousand thoughts went through his mind. There was no doubt now about the presence of Baron Gortz in the castle, since La Stilla was sequestered there.... It could only be he who was there.... La Stilla alive! ... But how would Franz reach her? ... How would he manage to drag her out of the castle? ... He did not know, but it had to happen... and it would happen.... The obstacles that Nic Deck had been unable to overcome, he would conquer.... It was not curiosity that was urging him into the midst of these ruins, but passion, his love for this woman whom he found alive, yes! alive! after believing she was dead, and he would snatch her away from Rudolf of Gortz!

Franz had told himself that he could win access only through the southern wall, where the barbican which led to the drawbridge was located. So, understanding that he didn't have to climb those high walls, he continued to walk along the crest of the Plateau of Orgall, as soon as he had turned the corner of the bastion.

During the day, that would not have offered any difficulties. In the dark of night, though, with the moon not yet risen—a night made dense with those mists that form in the mountains—it was more than hazardous. To the danger of stumbling, to the danger of toppling down to the bottom of the ditch, was added that of walking into rocks and perhaps causing a landslide.

But Franz kept going forward, hugging as close as possible to the zigzags of the counterscarp, groping with his hands and feet, so that he could be certain he wasn't getting lost. Supported by a superhuman strength, he felt guided too by an extraordinary instinct that could not deceive him.

Beyond the bastion the southern wall took shape, the one with which the drawbridge communicated when it wasn't raised against the barbican.

Beyond this bastion, obstacles seemed to multiply. Between the enormous rocks that were scattered all over the plateau, following the counterscarp was no longer practicable, and he had to walk away from it. Imagine a man trying to find his way around in the middle of a field in Carnac, where dolmens and menhirs were scattered haphazardly. And not one landmark by which to get his bearings, not one gleam of light in the dark night, which veiled everything right up to the top of the central keep!

But Franz continued to go forward, here hauling himself up onto an enormous block of stone that blocked his way, there crawling between the rocks, his hands torn by thistles and underbrush, his head grazed by a pair of white-tailed eagles, which fled as they emitted their horrible screeching cries.

Ah! Why didn't the old chapel's bell ring then as it had rung for Nic Deck and the doctor? Why didn't that intense light that had surrounded them light up over the crenellations of the keep? He could have walked toward that sound, he could have walked toward that light, like a sailor heading towards a warning siren or the light of a beacon!

No! ... Nothing but deep night, limiting the extent of his gaze to a few feet in front of him.

This went on for almost an hour. From the sloping ground he could feel at his left, Franz sensed he had wandered astray. Or had he descended lower down than the barbican? Perhaps he had overshot the drawbridge?

He stopped, feeling with his foot, wringing his hands. Which direction should he head? Rage overcame him at the thought that he might be forced to wait for daylight! ...And then he would be seen by the people of the castle... he wouldn't be able to surprise them.... Rudolf of Gortz would be on his guard....

It was at night, it was this very night that he had to penetrate the castle walls, and Franz couldn't manage to find his way in these shadows!

A cry escaped him... a cry of despair.

"Stilla..." he cried, "my Stilla!"

Did he think the prisoner could hear him, that she could answer him?

Nonetheless, twenty times over, he repeated this

name, which the echoes of the Plesa returned to him.

Suddenly something struck Franz's eyes. A gleam of light shone through the darkness—a bright light, which seemed to be coming from high above him.

"There is the castle... there!" he said to himself.

And, truly, from the position it occupied, this light could come only from the central keep.

Given his mental overexcitement, Franz was quick to think that it was La Stilla herself sending him this aid. No doubt about it, she had recognized him, at the moment he himself had glimpsed her on the terreplein of the bastion. And now it was she who was sending him this signal, it was she who was showing him the way he must follow to reach the barbican....

Franz headed towards this light, whose brightness increased as he approached it. Since he had gone too far to the left on the Plateau of Orgall, he was forced to climb back up about twenty feet to the right, and, after some groping attempts, he found again the edge of the counterscarp.

The light shone opposite him, and its height indeed proved that it came from one of the keep windows.

Franz was going to find himself faced with the last obstacles, then—perhaps insurmountable ones!

In fact, since the barbican was closed and the draw-bridge raised, he would have to let himself slide to the foot of the wall.... Then, what would he do in front of a wall that rose fifty feet above him?

Franz went towards the place which the drawbridge reached, when the barbican was open....

The drawbridge had been lowered.

Without even taking the time to reflect, Franz

crossed the shaky roadway of the drawbridge, and placed his hand on the door....

This door opened.

Franz hurried beneath the dark vault. But scarcely had he walked a few feet than the drawbridge clattered up against the barbican....

Count Franz of Telek was a prisoner in the Castle of the Carpathians.

XIII

The people of the Transylvanian countryside and the travelers who climb and descend the Vulkan Pass know what the Castle of the Carpathians looks like only from the outside. At the respectful distance at which fear halts the bravest people from the village of Werst and the surrounding area, it presents to the gaze only the enormous pile of stones of a ruined castle.

But, inside the enclosure, was the castle as dilapidated as we might suppose? No. In the shelter of its solid walls, the buildings of the old feudal fortress that had remained intact could still have housed an entire garrison.

Vast vaulted rooms; deep cellars; multiple passageways; courtyards whose stone paving vanished beneath tall thickets of grass; underground hideaways where daylight never penetrated; stairways hidden in the thick walls; blockhouses illumined by the narrow loopholes of the outer wall; the central keep with three floors, its chambers still adequately livable, crowned by a crenellated platform, between the various constructions of the enceinte; interminable hallways capriciously intertwining, rising up to the terreplein of the bastions, and descending into the bowels of the structure; here and there a few water tanks where rainwater was collected, the overflow from which ran down to the Nyad river; finally long tunnels, not blocked as people thought, which gave access to the road to the Vulkan Pass: such was the ensemble of the Castle of the Carpathians, whose geometrical layout offered a system that was as complicated as those of the labyrinths of Porsenna, Lemnos, or Crete.

Like Theseus wanting to conquer the daughter of Minos, it was an intense, irresistible feeling that had just drawn the young count through the endless meanderings of this castle. Would he find Ariadne's thread there, which guided the Greek hero?

Franz had only one thought: to penetrate this enclosure; and he had succeeded. Perhaps he should also have had this thought: that the drawbridge, which had been raised till that day, seemed to have been let down on purpose to let him pass! Perhaps he should have worried about the barbican suddenly closing behind him! But he hadn't even thought about it. He was finally inside this castle, where Rudolf of Gortz was keeping La Stilla, and he would sacrifice his life to reach her.

The gallery into which Franz had rushed, which was tall and wide and had a lowered ceiling, was plunged into the deepest darkness, and its uneven flagstones made it difficult to walk.

Franz went towards the left wall, and followed it by leaning on a facing covered with a deposit of niter that crumbled under his hand. He heard no sound except for that of his footsteps, which roused distant echoes. A warm current of air, laden with the stench of dilapidation, pushed him from behind, as if some in-draft had been created at the other end of this gallery.

After passing a stone pillar that buttressed the last corner on the left, Franz found himself at the entrance to a hallway that was perceptibly narrower. Just by stretching out his arms, he could touch the walls.

He went forward thus, his body bent over, groping with his feet and hands and trying to see if this hallway followed a straight line.

About two hundred feet from the corner pillar, Franz sensed that the hallway was bending to the left to take a completely opposite direction fifty feet further on. Did this hallway go back to the outer castle wall, or did it lead to the foot of the keep?

Franz tried to hasten his progress; but each time he was blocked, either by a rise in the ground level which made him stumble, or by a sudden turn that changed his direction. From time to time, he came across some opening, hollowed out of the wall, that led to the other buildings. But everything was dark, unfathomable, and in vain did he try to orient himself in the heart of this labyrinth, burrowing like a mole.

Franz must have turned round and retraced his steps many times, and realized he was losing his way in blind alleys. He had to be on his guard against some badly closed trap door giving way beneath his feet and casting him into the bottom of an oubliette, from which he could never be able to pull himself out. So when he walked upon some flooring that sounded hollow, he had to take care to keep to the wall, but still went forward with the same ardor that left him no time for reflection.

Still, since Franz had had neither to climb nor to descend, he still found himself on the level of the interior courtyards, which were spread out between the various buildings in the enclosure, and there was a chance that this hallway might end at the central keep, at the very place where the staircase began.

Unquestionably, a more direct method of communication must have existed between the barbican and the castle buildings. Surely during the years the Gortz family had lived there it could not have been necessary to walk through these interminable passageways. A second door, which faced the barbican opposite the first gallery, opened onto the place where the weapons were kept, in the midst of which the keep rose up; but it had been blocked up, and Franz hadn't even been able to recognize the place.

An hour went by during which the young count kept following the twists and turns, listening for some distant noise, not daring to shout the name La Stilla, which the echoes might have been able to carry up to the keep floors. He did not grow discouraged, though, and would have gone forward as long as he had strength, until some impassable obstacle forced him to stop.

However, without his realizing it, Franz was already exhausted. Since his departure from Werst, he had not eaten anything. He was suffering from hunger and thirst. His walk was uncertain, his legs weakening. In this humid, warm air that went through his clothing, his breath began to heave, and his heart beat quickly.

It must have been about nine o'clock when Franz, putting forward his left foot, didn't meet the ground.

He bent down, and his hand felt a step below, then another one.

There was a staircase there.

This staircase plunged into the foundations of the castle; perhaps it led nowhere?

Franz didn't hesitate. As he went down, he counted the steps, which set off at an angle to the hallway.

Seventy-seven steps led down to reach a second horizontal passageway, which was lost in multiple, dark windings.

Franz thus walked for the space of half an hour, and, broken with fatigue, he had just stopped, when a luminous point appeared two or three hundred feet in front of him.

Where did this light come from? Was it simply some natural phenomenon, hydrogen from a will-o'-the-wisp that had caught fire at this depth? Wasn't it really a lantern, being carried by one of the people who lived in the castle?

"Could it be she...?" Franz murmured.

And the thought occurred to him that once before a light had appeared, as if to show him the entrance to the castle, when he had gotten lost among the rocks on the Plateau of Orgall. If this was La Stilla who had showed him that light from one of the keep windows, wasn't it she again who was trying to guide him through the windings of this basement?

Scarcely master of himself, Franz kneeled down and

stared, without making any movement.

A diffuse clarity rather than a luminous point seemed to fill a kind of hypogeum at the end of the hallway.

Franz decided to hurry his way there by crawling, since his legs could barely support him anymore; and after going through a narrow opening, he fell onto the threshold of a crypt.

This crypt, in a good state of preservation, about twelve feet high, proved to be circular, of a regular dimensions. The ribs of its vault, which was supported by the capitals of eight bulbous pillars, radiated towards a pendentive keystone, in the center of which a glass phial was set, full of a yellowish light.

Opposite the door, between two of the pillars, there was another door, which was closed, and whose big nails, rust covering their heads, showed the place where the outer frameworks of bolts had been. Franz stood up, dragged himself to this second door, tried to shake it from its heavy jambs....

His efforts were useless.

Some dilapidated pieces of furniture were in the crypt; here, a bed, or rather a pallet made of old oak, on which miscellaneous bedding materials were scattered; there, a wooden stool with twisted feet, a table attached to the wall with iron tenons. On the table were various utensils, a large pitcher filled with water, a plate containing a piece of cold venison, a big round loaf of bread, like ship's biscuit. In a corner a basin was murmuring, fed by a trickle of water, the overflow from which ran in a funnel to the base of one of the pillars.

Didn't these arrangements, which had been made beforehand, indicate that a guest was expected in this crypt, or rather a prisoner in this prison? Was the prisoner Franz, then, and had he been drawn in by a trick?

In his confused state of mind, Franz didn't even have time for suspicion. Exhausted by hunger and fatigue, he devoured the food placed on the table and quenched his thirst with the contents of the pitcher; then he let himself fall across this coarse bed, where a few minutes' rest could return some of his strength to him.

But when he wanted to gather his thoughts, it seemed to him that they escaped him like water flowing from his hand.

Should he rather wait for daylight to recommence his search? Was his willpower so numb that he was no longer master of his actions?

"No!" he said to himself, "I will not wait! To the keep.... I have to reach the keep this very night!"

All of a sudden, the artificial light that the phial set into the keystone shed went out, and the crypt was plunged into complete darkness.

Franz wanted to get up.... He could not, and his thoughts went to sleep, or, to say it better, suddenly stopped, like the hand of a clock that had broken. It was a strange sleep, or rather an overwhelming torpor, an absolute annihilation of his being, which did not stem from peace of mind...,

How long this sleep had lasted, Franz could not tell, when he awoke. His watch, which had stopped, did not tell him the time. But the crypt was bathed once again in an artificial light.

Franz got out of his bed, took a few steps towards the first door: it was already open; towards the second door: it was still closed.

He wanted to think, but this was not easy to do.

Though his body had recovered from the fatigue of the previous day, his head felt both empty and heavy.

"How long was I asleep?" he wondered. "Is it night, or day?"

Inside the crypt, nothing was different, except that the light had been restored, the food replenished, and the pitcher refilled with clear water.

So someone must have entered while Franz had been plunged in that torpid stupor! They must know he had reached the inner depths of the castle! He was under the power of Baron Rudolf of Gortz.... Was he condemned to have no more communication with his fellows forever?

He could not accept that, and besides he would escape, since he could still do so; he would find again the gallery that led to the gate, he would leave the castle....

Leave? He remembered then that the barbican had closed behind him...

No matter! He would try to reach the outer wall, and through one of the openings in the wall, he would try to slip outside.... Come what may, before an hour went by he would have escaped the castle....

But La Stilla.... Would he give up trying to reach her? Would he leave without tearing her away from Rudolf of Gortz...?

No! And what he had been unable to bring to a close, he would finish with the help of the police agents that Rotzko must have brought back from Karlsburg to the village of Werst.... They would hurry to attack the old fortification.... They would search the castle from top to bottom!

Having taken this resolution, he had to put it into

execution without losing an instant.

Franz got up and was heading towards the hallway by which he had come in, when a kind of sliding sound came from behind the second door of the crypt.

He was sure that the noise was footsteps that were approaching—slowly.

Franz went to put his ear to the door, and, holding his breath, he listened....

The steps seemed to occur at regular intervals, as if they were climbing from one step to another. No doubt there was a second staircase there, which connected the crypt to the inner courtyards.

To be ready for any eventuality, Franz pulled the knife he was carrying in his belt out of its sheath and held it firmly in his hand.

If it was one of Baron Gortz's servants who entered, he would throw himself on top of him, snatch away his keys, keep him from being able to follow him; then, leaving through this new exit, he would try to reach the keep.

If it was Baron Rudolf of Gortz—and he would certainly recognize the man whom he had glimpsed when La Stilla fell onto the stage of the San Carlo—he would strike him without pity.

But the footsteps had stopped at the landing on the other side of the door.

Franz, not moving an inch, waited for the door to open....

It did not open, and a voice of infinite sweetness reached the young count.

It was the voice of La Stilla... yes! And her slightly tempered voice with all its inflections, its inexpressible charm, its caressing modulations, the admirable instrument of that wonderful art that seemed to have died along with the artist.

And La Stilla repeated the plaintive melody that had soothed Franz in his dream, when he was sleeping in the main room of the inn in Werst:

> Nel giardino de' mille fiori,
> Andiamo, mio cuore....

This song penetrated Franz to the deepest part of his soul.... He breathed it in, drank it like a divine liqueur, while La Stilla seemed to be inviting him to follow her, repeating:

> Andiamo, mio cuore...
> andiamo....

And yet the door did not open to let him pass! Couldn't he reach La Stilla, then, take her in his arms, drag her out of the castle...?

"Stilla... my Stilla...." he cried.

And he threw himself on the door, which resisted his efforts.

Already the song seemed to be weakening... the voice fading away... the footsteps growing distant....

Franz, kneeling, tried to shake the wood, tearing his hands on the hinges, still calling La Stilla, whose voice could just barely be heard.

Then a terrifying thought crossed his mind like a lightning bolt.

"Mad!" he cried, "She is mad, since she did not recognize me... since she did not answer me! ... Five years, locked up here... in the power of that man... my poor Stilla... she has lost her reason...."

Then he got up, his eyes haggard, his gestures disordered, his head on fire....

"Me too... I think my mind is wandering!" he repeated. "I think I am going mad... mad like her...."

He paced back and forth in the crypt in leaps, like a wild animal in its cage....

"No!" he repeated, "No! I cannot lose my head! I have to leave the castle.... I will leave it!"

And he rushed towards the first door....

It had just closed without a sound.

Franz hadn't noticed, while he was listening to La Stilla's voice....

After having been imprisoned inside the castle walls, now he was imprisoned in the crypt.

XIV

Franz was stunned. Just as he had feared, the ability to think, to understand things, the intelligence required to deduce their consequences, were little by little escaping him. The only feeling that persisted in him was the memory of La Stilla, the impression of that song that the echoes of that dark crypt no longer sent back to him.

Had he really been the victim of an illusion? No, a thousand times no! It was indeed La Stilla he had heard just now, and it was indeed she he had seen on the castle bastion.

Then that thought returned to him, the thought that she had lost her reason; that horrible realization struck him as if he had just lost her a second time.

"Mad!" he repeated to himself. "Yes! Mad... since she didn't recognize my voice... since she could not answer... mad... mad!"

And that was only too likely!

If he could only snatch her away from this castle, carry her off to his castle in Craiova, devote himself entirely to her, his care, his love could restore her reason to her!

That is what Franz was saying, prey to terrifying delirium; many hours went by before he had recovered possession of himself.

He tried then to reason coldly, to find his way in all the chaos of his thoughts.

"I must flee from here...." he said to himself. "How? As soon as they reopen this door! Yes! ...They came to replenish my provisions during my sleep.... I will wait.... I will pretend to sleep...."

Then a suspicion came to him: that the water of the pitcher must contain some kind of soporific substance.... If he had been plunged into that heavy sleep, in that complete annihilation whose duration he did not know, it was because he had drunk that water.... Well then, he would not drink any more of it.... He wouldn't even touch the food that had been placed on the table.... One of the people of the castle would come into the room, soon....

Soon?—What did he know about soon? At that moment, was the sun rising towards the zenith or setting on the horizon? Was it day or night?

So Franz tried to listen for the sound of a footstep, which might come close to one door or the other.... But when no sound reached him, he crawled along the crypt walls, his head burning, his eyes unfocussed, his ears humming, his breath heaving beneath the oppression of the atmosphere that had become heavier, and was scarcely renewed through the cracks in the doors.

Suddenly, at the corner of one of the right-hand pillars, he felt a cooler breath of air reach his lips.

Was there an opening in this place, then, by which a little air from outside could enter?

Yes... there was a passage that one wouldn't suspect under the shadow of the pillar.

In an instant the young count had slipped between the two walls and made for a rather dim light that seemed to come from above.

There a little courtyard opened up, five to six feet wide, whose walls rose to about a hundred feet. It was like the bottom of a well that served as an inner courtyard to this subterranean cell, and through which a little air and light came down.

So Franz could assure himself that it was still day. At the upper orifice of this well an angle of light was outlined, oblique at the level of the edge.

The sun must have finished at least half of its daily course, for this luminous angle tended to shrink.

It must have been about five o'clock in the evening.

All this entailed the consequence that Franz's sleep must have been prolonged for at least forty hours, and he had no doubt it had been provoked by a soporific drug.

So, since the young count and Rotzko had left the village of Werst the day before yesterday, June 11, it must be the day of the 13th that was just coming to an end....

As humid as the air was at the bottom of this courtyard, Franz breathed it in deeply, and felt a little relieved. But if he had hoped an escape might be possible through this long stone tube, he was soon convinced otherwise. To try to climb up along its walls, which offered no projections, was impossible.

Franz returned to the inside of the crypt. Since he could escape only through one of the two doors, he wanted to determine what sort of state they were in.

The first door—the one through which he had entered—was very solid, very thick, and must have been held on the outside by bolts slid into an iron strike plate, hence it was useless to try to force it open.

The second door—behind which La Stilla's voice had made itself heard—seemed less well preserved. The boards were flimsy in places.... Perhaps it wouldn't be too difficult to open a passage for himself on this side.

"Yes... that's the way... that's the way!" Franz said to himself, having recovered his calm.

But there was no time to lose, for it was probable that someone would enter the crypt, as soon as they thought he had fallen asleep under the influence of the sleep-inducing drink.

The work went faster than he could have hoped, since mildew had eaten away the wood around the metallic framework that held the bolts to the embrasure. With his knife, Franz managed to detach the round part, working almost noiselessly, pausing sometimes, listening, making sure he heard nothing outside.

Three hours later, the bolts were loose, and the door opened, creaking on its hinges.

Franz then went back out to the little courtyard, so that he could breathe less stifling air.

At that moment, the angle of light was no longer outlined at the orifice of the well, proof that the sun had already descended beneath Mt. Retyezat. The courtyard was plunged in profound darkness. Some stars shone through the oval coping, looking as they would through the tube of a long telescope. Little clouds went slowly by on the intermittent puffs from the breezes that were abating with nightfall. Certain tints in the atmosphere also indicated that the moon, still half full, had passed the horizon of the eastern mountains.

It must have been about nine o'clock in the evening.

Franz returned to take a little food and quench his thirst with the water from the basin, having first poured out the water in the pitcher. Then, attaching his knife to his belt, he went through the door, which he closed behind him.

Maybe now he would meet the unfortunate Stilla, wandering through these subterranean galleries...? At this thought, his heart beat as if it would break.

As soon as he had taken a few paces, he came against a step. Just as he had thought, a staircase began there, whose steps he counted as he climbed—just sixty, instead of the seventy-seven he must have descended to reach the threshold of the crypt. So there would have to be eight more for him to reach ground level.

Being able to think of nothing better, then, than to follow the dark hallway, whose walls he brushed with his outstretched hands, he continued to go forward.

Half an hour went by, without his being stopped by either a door or any bars. But many turns had kept him from reckoning his direction with respect to the outer wall, the one that faced the Plateau of Orgall.

After a few minutes' pause, during which he regained his breath, Franz began walking again, and it was beginning to seem as if this hallway was interminable when an obstacle stopped him.

It was a brick wall.

Feeling here and there at various heights, his hand did not encounter the slightest opening.

There was no way out on this side.

Franz could not hold back a cry. Any hope he had formed had broken against this obstacle. His knees bent, his legs gave way, he fell alongside the wall.

But, at ground level, the wall presented a narrow fissure, where the disjointed bricks barely adhered, and gave way beneath this fingers.

"That way... yes! That way!" Franz shouted.

And he began to remove the bricks one by one, when a noise could be heard on the other side.

Franz stopped.

The noise hadn't stopped, and, at the same time, a ray of light reached him through the fissure.

Franz looked.

It was the old chapel of the castle. What a lamentable state of dilapidation time and neglect had reduced it to: a half-collapsed vault, where a few ribs still joined over gibbous pillars; two or three ogival arches which seemed about to collapse; a broken window where flimsy mullions of flamboyant gothic style were outlined; here and there, a dusty marble slab, beneath which some ancestor of the Gortz family slept; in back of the chevet, a fragment of altar whose reredos showed scratched sculptures; then a remnant of roof crowning the top of the apse, which had been spared the gusts of wind, and finally, at the top of the portal, the rickety bell-tower, from which a rope hung to the ground—the rope of that bell which rang sometimes, to the inexpressible terror of the people of Werst who had lingered on the road to the pass.

Into this chapel, deserted for a long time, open to the bad weather of the Carpathian climate, a man had just come, holding a lantern in his hand, whose brightness cast his face in full light.

Franz immediately recognized this man.

It was Orfanik, the eccentric that the baron made his only companion during his stay in the great Italian cities, the peculiar character that people used to see walking through the streets, gesticulating and talking to himself, that misunderstood scholar, that inventor always in the pursuit of some chimera, and who was certainly placing his inventions at the service of Rudolf of Gortz!

If Franz had managed till then to preserve some doubt about the presence of the baron in the Castle of the Carpathians, even after the appearance of La Stilla, this doubt was changed into a certainty, since Orfanik was there in front of him.

What was he up to in this ruined chapel, at this late hour of the night?

Franz tried to find out, and this is what he saw quite clearly.

Orfanik, bent to the ground, had just lifted up several metal cylinders to which he attached a wire, which unrolled from a spool placed in a corner of the chapel. And such was the concentration he brought to this work that he would not even have seen the young count, if he had been in a position to do so.

Ah! Why wasn't the fissure that Franz had undertaken to enlarge not wide enough to let him pass! He could have entered the chapel, he could have rushed onto Orfanik, he would have forced him to lead him to the keep....

But perhaps it was fortunate that he was unable to do so, for, in case his attempt had failed, the Baron of Gortz would have made him pay with his life for the secrets he had just discovered!

A few minutes after Orfanik's arrival, another man entered the chapel.

It was Baron Rudolf of Gortz.

The unforgettable physiognomy of this person had not changed. He did not even seem to have aged, with his pale, long face that the lantern illumined from bottom to top, his long graying hair, thrown back, his gaze gleaming to the depths of his black eyes.

Rudolf of Gortz approached to examine the work Orfanik was performing.

And here are the words that were curtly exchanged between the two men.

XV

"Have you finished connecting the chapel, Orfanik?"

"I've just finished."

"Everything is ready in the blockhouses and bastions?"

"Everything."

"Are the bastions and chapel directly linked to the keep now?"

"They are."

"And, after the apparatus has switched on the current, we will have time to run away?"

"We will."

"Have you checked that the tunnel opening onto the Vulkan Pass is open?"

"It is."

Then there were a few moments of silence, while Orfanik, having taken up his lantern again, directed its brightness into the depths of the chapel.

"Ah! Old castle of mine," the baron cried, "you will make them pay dearly if they try to force their way into your bounds!"

And Rudolf of Gortz uttered these words in a tone that made the young count tremble.

"Have you heard what they're saying in Werst?" he asked Orfanik.

"Fifty minutes ago, the wire brought me what was being said in the King Mathias inn."

"Is the attack set for tonight?"

"No, it won't take place till sunrise."

"How long ago did Rotzko return to Werst?"

"Two hours ago, with the police agents he brought back from Karlsburg."

"Well then! Since the castle can no longer defend itself," Baron Gortz repeated, "at least it will crush that Franz of Telek beneath its rubble, along with all those who come to his aid."

Then, after a few moments:

"And this wire, Orfanik?" he went on. "No one must ever know it established a communication between the castle and the village of Werst...."

"They will not find out; I will destroy this wire."

In our opinion, the time has come to give an explanation for certain phenomena that occurred during the course of this narrative, and whose origin should now be revealed.

At that time—we will emphasize the fact that this story occurred in one of the last years of the nineteenth

century—the use of electricity, which is rightly considered "the soul of the universe," had just been finally per-
fected. The illustrious Edison and his disciples had completed their work.

Among other electric appliances, the telephone func-
tioned then with such a wonderful precision that sounds,
collected by plates, reached the ear freely without the
help of ear-trumpets. Whatever was said, whatever was
sung, whatever was even whispered, one could hear
regardless of the distance, and two people, separated by
thousands of leagues, chatted to each other as if they had
been sitting opposite each other.[*]

For many years already, Orfanik, the inseparable
companion of Baron Rudolf of Gortz, was a first-rate
inventor in matters concerning the practical use of electricity. But, as we know, his admirable discoveries had
not been welcomed as they deserved. The scholarly
world had decided to view him as a mere madman, rather
than a man of genius in his art. That was the source of
the implacable hatred that the inventor, rejected and
rebuffed, had conceived for his colleagues.

It was in that condition that Baron Gortz met
Orfanik, gnawed by misery. The baron encouraged his
labors, opened his purse to him, and, finally, allowed him
to become his associate—provided, of course, that the
scholar reserved the benefit of his inventions exclusively
for him, so that he alone would profit from them.

On the whole, these two characters, each one eccentric and fanatic in his own way, were well suited to get
along with each other. Since their first meeting, then,
they had never separated—not even when Baron Gortz
followed La Stilla through all the cities in Italy.

[*] They could even see each other in mirrors relayed by
the wires, thanks to the invention of the telephone.

But, while the music-lover was becoming intoxicated by the incomparable artist's singing, Orfanik was busy only with perfecting the discoveries in electricity that had been made by scientists during these last few years, perfecting their applications, and getting the most extraordinary results from them.

After the incidents that terminated the tragic career of La Stilla, Baron Gortz disappeared without anyone knowing what had become of him. In fact, when he left Naples, he had gone to take refuge in the Castle of the Carpathians, accompanied by Orfanik, who was quite satisfied at being immured there with him.

When he had taken the resolution to hide his existence within the walls of this old castle, Baron Gortz's intention was that no inhabitant of the countryside should suspect his return, and that no one be tempted to visit him. It goes without saying that Orfanik and he had quite sufficient means to assure their material life in the castle. There was a secret access to the road to the Vulkan Pass, and it was by this road that a trustworthy man, a former servant of the baron's whom no one knew, brought whatever was needed for the existence of Baron Rudolf and his companion at pre-arranged dates.

Actually, what remained of the castle—especially the central keep—was less dilapidated than people thought, and even more inhabitable than the needs of its guests required. Thus, provided with whatever was necessary for his experiments, Orfanik was able to undertake these prodigious labors for which physics and chemistry provided him the elements. And then the idea came to him to use them with the aim of frightening away unwelcome visitors.

Baron Gortz welcomed the proposition with enthusiasm, and Orfanik installed a special machine, created to terrify the countryside by producing phenomena that could only be attributed to diabolical intervention.

But above all, Baron Gortz wanted to be kept informed of what was being said in the nearest village. Was there a way to hear people talking without their suspecting? Yes, if one managed to establish a telephonic communication between the castle and that main room in the King Mathias inn, where the foremost members of Werst were accustomed to meet every night.

Orfanik accomplished this both cleverly and secretly in the simplest way. A copper wire, covered in its insulating sheath, one end of which went up to the first floor of the keep, was unrolled under the Nyad river as far as the village of Werst. Once he had completed this first task, Orfanik, passing himself off as a tourist, came to spend a night in the King Mathias, so that he could connect this wire to the main room of the inn. It is easy to see that it was not difficult for him to bring the end of the wire out of the riverbed and up to that rear window which was never opened. Then, having placed a telephonic apparatus there, hidden by the thick foliage, he attached the wire to it. Now, since this apparatus was wonderfully placed to emit as well as gather sounds, it followed that Baron Gortz was able to hear everything that was said in the King Mathias, and also to make whatever he liked heard through it.

During the first years, the tranquility of the castle was not disturbed in the least. The bad reputation it enjoyed was enough to keep the inhabitants of Werst away. Moreover, everyone knew it was abandoned after the death of the last family servants. But, one day, in the time when this tale begins, the telescope of the shepherd Frik allowed him to see a plume of smoke that was escaping from one of the keep chimneys. Starting from that instant, people started talking even more, and we know what the result was.

It was then that the telephonic communication proved useful, since Baron Gortz and Orfanik could be kept up to date about what was happening in Werst. It was by means of the wire that they found out about the resolution Nic Deck had made to go to the castle, and it was by means of the wire that a threatening voice suddenly made itself heard in the King Mathias taproom to dissuade him. Later, since the young forester persisted in his resolution despite this threat, Baron Gortz decided to inflict such a lesson on him that he would lose any desire ever to return there. That night, Orfanik's machinery, which was ready to function then, produced a series of phenomena stemming from pure physics, of a sort to throw the surrounding countryside into terror: the bell ringing in the chapel's campanile; the projection of intense flames mixed with sea salt, which gave all objects a spectral appearance; formidable sirens from which compressed air escaped in terrifying roars; photographic silhouettes of monsters projected by means of powerful reflectors; plates arranged in the weeds in the trench of the enclosure and made to communicate with batteries whose current had seized the doctor by his hobnailed boots; finally an electric discharge, released by batteries in the laboratory, which had knocked down the forester the instant his hand came to rest on the drawbridge hinge.

Just as Baron Gortz had expected, after the appearance of these inexplicable wonders, after Nic Deck's attempt had turned out so badly, terror was at its height, and no one would have cared, for either gold or silver, to come within even two miles of the Castle of the Carpathians, which was obviously haunted by supernatural beings.

So Rudolf of Gortz must have thought he was safe from any unwelcome curiosity, when Franz of Telek arrived in the village of Werst.

While he was questioning Jonas, or Master Koltz or the others, his presence at the King Mathias inn was immediately made known by the wire under the Nyad. The hatred of Baron Gortz for the young count was rekindled with the memory of the events that had occurred in Naples. And not only was Franz of Telek in the village, a few miles away from the castle, but now he was making light of their absurd superstitions, in front of the noteworthy members of the village; he was demolishing that fantastic reputation that protected the Castle of the Carpathians; he was even undertaking to tell the Karlsburg authorities, so that the police would come put an end to all these legends!

Thus Baron Gortz resolved to draw Franz of Telek to the castle, and we know by what various means he succeeded. The voice of La Stilla, sent to the King Mathias inn through the telephonic apparatus, had provoked the young count to make a detour to approach the castle; the appearance of the singer on the terreplein of the bastion had given him the irresistible desire to enter it; a light, shown at one of the keep windows, had guided him to the barbican which was open to let him through. At the bottom of that crypt, illumined electrically, from which he had again heard that penetrating voice, between the walls of that cell, where food was brought to him while he slept a lethargic sleep, in that prison buried beneath the depths of the castle whose door had closed on him, Franz of Telek was under the power of Baron Gortz, and Baron Gortz was counting on his never being able to leave it.

Such were the results obtained by this mysterious collaboration between Rudolf of Gortz and his accomplice Orfanik. But, to his great vexation, the baron knew that the alarm had been given by Rotzko who, not having followed his master inside the castle, had told the Karlsburg authorities. A squad of police agents had arrived at the village of Werst, and Baron Gortz was going to have to deal with too strong a contingent. In fact, how would Orfanik and he manage to defend themselves against such a numerous troop? The means used against Nic Deck and Dr. Patak would be insufficient, for the police did not believe in diabolical interventions. Thus both of them had decided to destroy the castle from top to bottom, and they were now just waiting for the moment to act. An electrical current was prepared to set fire to the charges of dynamite that had been buried beneath the keep, the bastions, and the old chapel, and the apparatus, made to start this current, would leave Baron Gortz and his accomplice enough time to flee through the tunnel to the Vulkan Pass. Then, after the explosion of which the young count and a number of those who had climbed the castle wall would be victims, both would have hidden themselves so far away that they would never be found.

What he had just heard in this conversation had provided Franz with an explanation for the phenomena that had occurred in the past. Now he knew that a telephonic communication existed between the Castle of the Carpathians and the village of Werst. He also knew that the castle was going to be destroyed in a catastrophe that would cost him his life and would be fatal to the agents of police brought by Rotzko. Finally, he knew that Baron Gortz and Orfanik would have time to flee—to flee, bringing La Stilla with them, unaware....

Why couldn't Franz force his way into the chapel and hurl himself on these two men! ...He could have knocked them to the floor, struck them, neutralized them, he could have prevented the terrible destruction of the castle!

But what was impossible now might not be so after the baron's departure. When both of them had left the chapel, Franz, hurrying in their footsteps, would follow them to the keep, and, with God's help, he would take care of them!

Baron Gortz and Orfanik were already in the rear of the chevet. Franz did not lose sight of them. What exit would they go through? Would it be a door opening onto one of the courtyards in the close, or would it be some inner hallway that had to connect the chapel to the keep, since it seemed that all the castle buildings communicated with each other? It didn't matter, so long as the young count didn't run up against an obstacle he couldn't overcome.

At that moment, some words were again exchanged between Baron Gortz and Orfanik.

"There is nothing more to do here?"

"Nothing."

"Then let us separate."

"Your wish is still that I leave you alone in the castle...?"

"Yes, Orfanik, and leave immediately through the tunnel to the Vulkan Pass."

"But you...?"

"I will leave the castle only at the last instant."

"It is settled that I should go to Bistritz to wait for you?"

"Yes, to Bistritz."

"Then stay, Baron Rudolf, and stay alone, since that is your will."

"Yes... for I want to hear her.... I want to hear her one more time during this final night I spend in the Castle of the Carpathians!"

A few more instants and Baron Gortz, with Orfanik, had left the chapel.

Although the name of La Stilla had not been uttered in this conversation, Franz had understood that it was she about whom Rudolf of Gortz had just spoken.

XVI

Disaster was imminent. Franz could only prevent it by making it impossible for Baron Gortz to carry out his plan.

It was eleven o'clock at night. No longer fearing discovery, Franz resumed his work. The bricks in the wall came out quite easily; but its thickness was such that half an hour went by before the opening was large enough to let him through.

As soon as Franz had set foot inside this chapel open to the elements, he felt revived by the air from outside. Through the gaps in the nave and the window embrasures, wispy clouds could be seen in the sky, chased by the breeze. Here and there some stars appeared, made pale by the brilliance of the moon rising over the horizon.

Franz had to find the door that opened in the back of the chapel, through which Baron Gortz and Orfanik had gone out. For this reason, having crossed the nave diagonally, Franz made for the chevet.

In this utterly dark section, where the moon's rays did not penetrate, he stumbled against the rubble from tombs and on fragments that had fallen from the archway.

Finally, at the extreme end of the chevet, behind the reredos of the altar, near a dark corner, Franz felt a worm-eaten door give way as he pushed it.

This door opened onto a gallery, which must have run the length of the close.

It was through it that Baron Gortz and Orfanik had entered the chapel, and it was through it that they had just left.

As soon as Franz was inside the gallery, he found himself once again immersed in complete darkness. After a number of detours, without having either to climb or descend, he was certain he had had remained at the level of the inner courtyards.

Half an hour later, the darkness seemed to be less profound: a faint light slipped through some side openings in the gallery.

Franz could walk more quickly, and he ended up in a wide blockhouse, situated beneath the terreplein of the bastion, which flanked the left corner of the outer walls.

This blockhouse was pierced with narrow loopholes, through which the moon's rays penetrated.

Across from this there was an open door.

Franz's first concern was to stand in front of one of these loopholes, so that he could breathe the cool night breeze for a few seconds.

But, the instant he was about to withdraw, he thought he glimpsed two or three shadows which were moving at the lower end of the Plateau of Orgall, illumined as far as the dark mass of the forest.

Franz looked.

Some men were walking back and forth on this plateau, a little in front of the trees—no doubt the police agents from Karlsburg, brought by Rotzko. Had they decided to work at night, then, in the hope of surprising the inhabitants of the castle, or were they waiting in that place for the first light of dawn?

What an effort Franz had to exercise on himself to hold back the cry that was ready to escape from him, not to call Rotzko, who would have heard him and recognized his voice! But this cry could reach the keep, and, before the police agents had climbed the wall, Rudolf of Gortz would have the time to switch on his apparatus and flee through the tunnel.

Franz managed to gain control of himself and walk away from the loophole. Then, after crossing the blockhouse, he went through the door and continued to follow the gallery.

Five hundred steps further on, he reached the entrance to a staircase that led into the thick wall.

Had he finally come to the keep that stood in the middle of the arsenal? He had reason to believe so.

However, this staircase must not have been the main staircase that led to the various floors. It was comprised of only one series of circular steps, arranged like the threads of a screw inside a narrow, dark cage.

Franz climbed noiselessly, listening, but hearing nothing, and, after about twenty steps, he stopped on a landing.

There, a door opened, leading to a terrace, which surrounded the keep on its second floor.

Franz glided along this terrace and, taking care to take shelter behind the parapet, he looked in the direction of the Plateau of Orgall.

Many men could still be seen at the edge of the forest, and there was no indication that they planned to approach the castle.

Having made up his mind to catch up with Baron Gortz before he had fled through the tunnel to the pass, Franz skirted round the floor and arrived at another door, where the corkscrew of the staircase resumed its upward turnings.

He set foot on the first step, leaned both hands on the walls, and began to climb.

Still the same silence.

The second floor apartment was not inhabited.

Franz hurried to reach the landings that gave access to the upper floors.

When he had reached the third floor, his foot did not encounter any more steps. The staircase ended here, on this floor that housed the highest apartment in the keep, the one that crowned the crenellated platform, where the standard of the barons of Gortz used to fly.

The wall to the left of the landing was pierced with a door, which was now closed.

Through the keyhole, whose key was on the outside, a bright ray of light filtered.

Franz listened and could not hear any noise inside the apartment.

Applying his eye to the lock, he could make out only the left part of a room, which was very bright; the right part was plunged in darkness.

After quietly turning the key, Franz pushed the door,

which opened.

A spacious room occupied this entire upper floor of the keep. Mounted on its circular walls was a coffered vault, whose ribs, meeting in the center, merged in a heavy pendentive. Thick hangings, old tapestries with figures on them, covered its walls. Some old furniture—sideboards, dressers, armchairs, stools—furnished it rather artistically. At the windows hung thick drapes, which let none of the brightness inside pass outside. On the floor was a thick wool rug, on which footsteps were muffled.

The arrangement of the room was peculiar at the very least, and, entering it, Franz was especially struck by the contrast it offered, depending on whether it was bathed in shadow or in light.

To the right of the door, the back of the room disappeared into a profound darkness.

To the left, though, a platform draped with black cloth received a powerful light, owing to some concentrating apparatus placed in front of it, but in such a way that it could not itself be seen.

A dozen feet from this platform, from which it was separated by a screen at chest height, was an old tall-backed armchair, which the screen surrounded with a kind of penumbra.

Near the armchair, a small table, covered with a cloth, supported a rectangular box.

This box, about twelve to fifteen inches long, and five to six inches wide, whose cover, encrusted with gems, was raised, contained a metal cylinder.

As soon as Franz entered the room, he saw that the armchair was occupied.

In it, in fact, there was a person who preserved a complete immobility, his head upturned against the back of the armchair, his eyelids closed, his right arm stretched out on the table, his hand leaning on the front part of the box.

It was Rudolf of Gortz.

Was it so that he could abandon himself to sleep that the baron had wanted to spend this last night on the uppermost floor of the old keep?

No! That could not be, according to what Franz had heard him say to Orfanik.

Baron Gortz was alone in this room, moreover, and, in keeping with the orders he had received, it was certain that his companion had already fled through the tunnel.

And La Stilla...? Hadn't Rudolf of Gortz also said that he wanted to hear her one last time in this Castle of the Carpathians, before it was destroyed by the explosion? And for what other reason would he have come back to this room, where she must have come, every evening, to intoxicate him with her singing...?

Where was La Stilla, then?

Franz did not see her and did not hear her....

After all, what did it matter, now that Rudolf of Gortz was at the mercy of the young count! Franz would soon be able to force him to speak. But, given the state of overexcitement in which he found himself, wasn't he going to hurl himself on this man whom he hated as he was hated by him, by the man who had taken La Stilla away from him.... La Stilla, alive and mad... mad because of him... and strike him?

Franz came to take up his position behind the armchair. He just had one step to take to seize Baron Gortz,

and, with blood throbbing in his veins, his head exploding, he raised his hand....

Suddenly La Stilla appeared.

Franz let his knife fall onto the rug.

La Stilla was standing on the platform, bathed in
light, her hair flowing, her arms stretched out, wonderfully beautiful in her white costume of Angelica in
Orlando, just as she had shown herself on the bastion of
the castle. Her eyes, fixed on the young count, penetrated him to the depths of his soul....

It was impossible that Franz couldn't be seen by her,
and yet, La Stilla did not make a gesture to call him...
she did not open her lips to speak to him.... Alas! She
was mad!

Franz was about to rush onto the platform to seize
her in his arms, to drag her outside....

La Stilla had just begun to sing. Without leaving his
armchair, Baron Gortz was leaning towards her. In a
paroxysm of ecstasy, the dilettante breathed in this voice
like a perfume, he drank it in like a divine liqueur. Just
as he was before, at the performances in the Italian theaters, just so was he now, in the midst of this room in an
infinite solitude, at the top of this keep that dominated
the Transylvanian countryside!

Yes! La Stilla was singing! She was singing for him...
only for him! It was like a breath exhaling from her lips,
which seemed to be motionless.... But, if reason had
abandoned her, at least her artist's soul was still left to
her, intact!

Franz too was intoxicated by the charm of this voice,
which he hadn't heard in five long years.... He was
absorbed in the ardent contemplation of this woman

whom he thought he would never see again, and who was there, living, as if some miracle had resuscitated her for his eyes!

And this song of La Stilla's, wasn't it the one song among all others that could make the cords of memory vibrate most strongly in Franz's heart? Yes! He had recognized the finale of the tragic scene in *Orlando*, that finale when the singer's soul had been broken in this last phrase:

> Innamorata, mio cuore tremante,
> Voglio morire....

Franz followed it note by note, that ineffable phrase.... And he said to himself that it had never been interrupted, as it had been on the San Carlo stage! No! It would not die in the lips of La Stilla, as she had died at her farewell performance....

Franz stopped breathing.... His entire life was attached to this song.... A few more measures, and the song would be finished in all its incomparable purity....

But now the voice began to weaken.... It was as if La Stilla were hesitating, as she repeated these words of poignant suffering:

> Voglio morire....

Would La Stilla fall on this platform as she fell before onto the stage...?

She did not fall, but the song stopped at the same bar, at the same note as at the Teatro San Carlo.... She let out a cry... and it was the same cry that Franz had heard that night....

And yet, La Stilla was still there, standing, motionless, with her beloved gaze—that gaze that ignited all the tenderness of his soul in the young count...

Franz rushed towards her.... He wanted to carry her outside of this room, outside of this castle....

At that instant, he found himself face to face with the baron, who had just gotten up.

"Franz of Telek!" Rudolf of Gortz cried. "Franz of Telek, who was able to escape...."

But Franz did not even reply, and, rushing towards the platform:

"Stilla... my dear Stilla," he said over and over, "I find you here... alive...."

"Alive.... La Stilla... alive!" Baron Gortz cried.

And this ironic phrase ended in a burst of laughter, in which all the fury of rage could be heard.

"Living!" Rudolf of Gortz went on. "Well then! Let Franz of Telek try to take her away from me!"

Franz stretched out his arms towards La Stilla, whose eyes were passionately fixed on him...

At that instant, Rudolf of Gortz bent down, picked up the knife that had fallen from Franz's hand, and made for the motionless Stilla....

Franz rushed onto him, to deflect the blow that threatened the unfortunate madwoman...

It was too late... the knife struck her heart....

Suddenly, the noise of a mirror breaking was heard, and, with the thousand shards of glass scattered throughout the room, La Stilla disappeared....

Franz remained inert.... He didn't understand.... Had he, too, become mad?

And then Rudolf of Gortz cried out:

"La Stilla still escapes Franz of Telek! But her voice.... her voice remains with me.... Her voice is mine... mine alone... and will never belong to anyone else!"

At the instant when Franz was going to throw himself on Baron Gortz, his strength left him, and he fell unconscious at the foot of the platform.

Rudolf of Gortz did not even take heed of the young count. He seized the box that was on the table, hurried out of the room, went down to the keep's second floor; then, having reached the terrace, he skirted round it, and was about to reach the other door, when a shot resounded.

Rotzko, posted at the edge of the counterscarp, had just fired at Baron Gortz.

The baron was not hit, but Rotzko's bullet shattered the box he was holding in his arms.

He let out a terrible cry.

"Her voice... her voice!" he repeated. "Her soul... the soul of La Stilla.... It is broken... broken... broken!"

And then, his hair standing on end, his hands clasped, he ran along the terrace, still crying out:

"Her voice... her voice! They have broken her voice! A curse on all of them!"

Then he disappeared through the door, at the instant that Rotzko and Nic Deck were trying to climb the castle wall, without waiting for the police squad. Almost immediately, an immense explosion rocked the entire massif of the Plesa. A burst of flames rose to the clouds, and an avalanche of stones fell onto the road to Vulkan.

Of the bastions, the outer wall, the keep, the chapel of the Castle of the Carpathians, there remained only a mass of smoking ruins on the surface of the Plateau of Orgall.

XVII

We have not forgotten, harking back to the conversation between the Baron and Orfanik, that the explosion was supposed to destroy the castle only after the departure of Rudolf of Gortz. Yet at the moment the explosion occurred, it would not have been possible for the baron to have had the time to flee through the tunnel to reach the road to the pass. In the passion of his suffering, in the madness of his despair, no longer aware of what he was doing, had Rudolf of Gortz provoked an instantaneous catastrophe of which he must have been the first victim? After the incomprehensible words that had sprung from his lips the instant Rotzko's bullet had smashed the box he was carrying, had he wanted to bury himself beneath the ruins of the castle?

In any case, it was very fortunate that the police, surprised by Rotzko's rifle shot, were still some distance away when the explosion shook the massif. A few of them were slightly grazed by the debris falling onto the surface of the Plateau of Orgall. Only Rotzko and the forester had reached the bottom of the wall by then, and it was truly a miracle that they had not been crushed beneath that hail of stones.

So the explosion had produced its effects when Rotzko, Nic Deck, and the police managed, without too much difficulty, to get through the wall by climbing the ditch, which had been half filled-in by the collapse of the walls.

Fifty feet beyond the outer wall, a body was found in the midst of the rubble, at the base of the keep.

It was the body of Rudolf of Gortz. Some old inhabitants of the region—Master Koltz, among others—recognized him without hesitation.

As for Rotzko and Nic Deck, they were thinking only of finding the young count. Since Franz had not reappeared in the length of time he had agreed with his soldier, it must have been because he had been unable to escape the castle.

But Rotzko did not dare to hope his master had survived and had not been a victim of the catastrophe; the man was crying copiously, and Nic Deck did not know how to calm him.

However, after half an hour of searching, the young count was found on the keep's second floor, beneath the wall's flying buttress, which had prevented him from being crushed.

"My Master... my poor master...."

"Your Excellency..."

These were the first words that Rotzko and Nic

Duck uttered, when they leaned over Franz. They must have thought he was dead, while in fact he had only fainted.

Franz opened his eyes; but his wandering gaze seemed neither to recognize Rotzko nor to hear him.

Nic Deck, who had lifted up the young count in his arms, spoke to him again; he made no reply.

Only these last words of La Stilla's song escaped from his lips:

Innamorata.... Voglio morire....

Franz of Telek was mad.

XVIII

Since the young count had lost his reason, probably no one would ever have learned the true explanation of the final events of which the Castle of the Carpathians had been the theater, if it had not been for the revelations that came about in the following circumstances.

For four days, Orfanik had waited, as agreed, for Baron Gortz to come join him in the town of Bistritz. When he did not see him reappear, he began to wonder if the Baron had been a victim of the explosion. Urged by curiosity then as much as by anxiety, he had left the town, taken the road to Werst again, and returned to wander about the environs of the castle.

Ill fortune befell him, since the police were quick to seize him under Rotzko's orders, who had recognized him.

Once in the capital of the region, in the presence of

the investigating magistrates before whom he was led, Orfanik readily answered the questions that were put to him in the course of the investigation of this catastrophe.

We will even confess that the sad end of Baron Rudolf of Gortz did not seem to affect this egotistical and maniacal scholar, who held nothing but his inventions close to his heart.

In the first place, to Rotzko's pressing questions, Orfanik confirmed that La Stilla was dead, and—these are the terms he used—that she had been buried, and buried well, for five years in the cemetery of the Campo Santo Nuovo, in Naples.

This assertion was not the least of the surprises this strange adventure would provoke.

In fact, if La Stilla was dead, how was it that Franz could have heard her voice in the main room of the inn, and then have seen her appear on the terreplein of the bastion, and then have become intoxicated by her singing, when he was locked in the crypt? ... Finally, how had he found her alive in the room in the keep?

Here is the explanation for these various phenomena, which seemed to be inexplicable.

We remember what despair had seized Baron Gortz when he heard the rumor had been spread that La Stilla had resolved to abandon the operatic stage to become the Countess of Telek. The baron would miss the artist's admirable talent, that is to say all the satisfactions his dilettante's soul derived from it.

It was then that Orfanik proposed to him to gather, by means of phonographic apparatuses, the principal numbers from her repertoire, which the singer was to sing during her farewell performances. These machines were already wonderfully developed by that time, and Orfanik had made them so perfect that the human voice underwent no alteration whatsoever, neither in its charm, nor in its purity.

Baron Gortz accepted the physicist's offer. Phonographs were installed one after the other, secretly, in the back of the barred loge during the final months of the season. Thus there were engraved on their plates the singer's cavatinas, art songs, and opera arias; among others, there was Stefano's melody, and that final air from *Orlando* that was interrupted by La Stilla's death.

Those are the conditions in which Baron Gortz had come to lock himself up in the Castle of the Carpathians, where, every night, he could hear the songs that had been collected by these admirable machines. Not only could he hear La Stilla as if he had been in his loge, but—which can seem absolutely incomprehensible—he could see her as if she were alive, in front of his eyes.

It was a simple optical illusion.

We have not forgotten that Baron Gortz had acquired a magnificent portrait of the singer. This portrait represented her life-size, wearing her white costume as Angelica in *Orlando*, with all her magnificent flowing hair. Now, by means of mirrors curved according to a certain angle calculated by Orfanik, when a powerful light illumined this portrait placed before a mirror, La Stilla appeared, in reflection, as "real" as when she was full of life and in all the splendor of her beauty. It was thanks to this apparatus, carried during the night onto the terre-plein of the bastion, that Rudolf of Gortz had made her appear, when he had wanted to draw Franz of Telek in; it was thanks to this same apparatus that the young count had seen La Stilla again in the room in the keep, while his fanatical admirer was intoxicated by her voice and her songs.

Such is, in brief, the information that Orfanik provided in greater detail during the course of his interrogation. And, it should be said, it was with an unequalled pride that he declared he was author of these wonderful inventions, which he had brought to their highest degree of perfection.

However, though Orfanik had explained these various phenomena—or rather these "tricks," to use the usual word—from a material point of view, what he did not explain was why Baron Gortz, before the explosion, had not had the time to flee through the tunnel to the Vulkan Pass. But once Orfanik learned that a bullet had smashed the object that Rudolf of Gortz was carrying in his arms, he understood. This object was the phonographic apparatus that contained La Stilla's last song; it was the one that Rudolf of Gortz had wanted to hear one last time in the room in the keep, before its collapse. Once this apparatus was destroyed, Baron Gortz's life was destroyed too, and, mad with despair, he had chosen to be buried beneath the ruins of his castle.

The Baron Rudolf of Gortz was buried in the cemetery in Werst with the honors due to the ancient family that ended with him. As to the young Count of Telek, Rotzko had him conveyed back to the castle in Craiova, where he devoted himself wholly to caring for his master. Orfanik willingly handed over to him the phonographs on which the other songs of La Stilla were collected, and, when Franz heard the great artist's voice, he gave it some of his attention, and regained some of his lucidity from before; it seemed as if his soul were trying to come to life again in the memories of this unforgettable past.

In fact, a few months later, the young count had recovered his reason, and it was through him that they learned the details of that last night in the Castle of the Carpathians.

Let us say now that the wedding of the charming Miriota and Nic Deck was celebrated in the week or so following the catastrophe. After the newlyweds had received the blessing of the priest in the village of Vulkan, they returned to Werst, where Master Koltz had reserved the most beautiful room in his house for them.

But, although all these strange events had been given natural explanations, we shouldn't for a moment imagine that the young woman no longer believed in the fantastic apparitions of the castle. Nic Deck tried to reason with her in vain—Jonas too, since he was eager to bring customers back to the King Mathias; she was not convinced, no more than Master Koltz, the shepherd Frik, Magister Hermod, or the other inhabitants of Werst. Many years would go by, probably, before these fine people renounced their superstitious beliefs.

Still, Dr. Patak, who had resumed his usual boasts, kept repeating to whoever would listen:

"Well then! Didn't I say so? ... Spirits in the castle! ... As if spirits existed!"

But no one listened to him, and people even asked him to be quiet, since his mockery was uncivil.

For the rest, Magister Hermod continued to base his lessons on the study of Transylvanian legends. For a long time to come, the young generation of the village of Werst will believe that spirits from the other world haunt the ruins of the Castle of the Carpathians.